"All you got to do is tell me where your brother's things are. That's all I need from you, lady."

The door burst open.

Andrew entered with his gun drawn. "Let her go."

The man placed his pistol on Hope's heart.

"The police will be here any minute," Andrew warned him. "Let her go and this will all go more smoothly for you."

"I don't believe you," the man said. His free hand went to the back of Hope's neck. He was close enough to her that she could hear his shallow, uneven breathing and smell his sweat.

"Put the gun down and step away from her." Andrew's voice remained strong and authoritative.

"Please," she said. "I can see you're not a killer."

The pressure on her chest let up slightly, and she thought he was going to toss the gun. Instead, the man moved it to her head so he could step behind her and use her as a shield. He pulled her backward.

Andrew took a step closer.

"Take a shot. Maybe you'll hit her or maybe you'll hit me."

Ever since she found the Nancy Drew books with the pink covers in her country school library, **Sharon Dunn** has loved mystery and suspense. Most of her books take place in Montana, where she lives with three nearly grown children and a hyper border collie. She lost her beloved husband of twenty-seven years to cancer in 2014. When she isn't writing, she loves to hike surrounded by God's beauty.

Books by Sharon Dunn

Love Inspired Suspense

Fatal Vendetta
Big Sky Showdown
Hidden Away
In Too Deep
Wilderness Secrets
Mountain Captive
Undercover Threat
Alaskan Christmas Target
Undercover Mountain Pursuit
Crime Scene Cover-Up
Christmas Hostage
Montana Cold Case Conspiracy
Montana Witness Chase

Alaska K-9 Unit

Undercover Mission

Pacific Northwest K-9 Unit

Threat Detection

Visit the Author Profile page at LoveInspired.com for more titles.

MONTANA WITNESS CHASE

SHARON DUNN

LOVE INSPIRED SUSPENSE
INSPIRATIONAL ROMANCE

LOVE INSPIRED® SUSPENSE
INSPIRATIONAL ROMANCE

ISBN-13: 978-1-335-59927-8

Recycling programs
for this product may
not exist in your area.

Montana Witness Chase

Be strong and of a good courage;
be not afraid, neither be thou dismayed:
for the Lord thy God is with thee whithersoever thou goest.
—*Joshua* 1:9

This book is dedicated to my readers, whose encouragement and positive feedback keep me writing.

ONE

Andrew Lewis stared through the w.Marshal of his car at the throngs of people wandering the sidewalk and closed-off streets of downtown Whitetail, Montana.

Hope Miller, the woman in witness protection that he'd been assigned to escort to her new location, sat up straighter in the passenger seat. "It's an art walk. I read about it in the guidebook I asked for about this part of Montana when I found out this was where I was going to be placed. They do them on the second Friday of every month all summer."

He tightened his grip on the wheel. Anytime he was transporting a witness, two things put him on edge: crowds and the unexpected delays. Now he was dealing with both. "Looks like I'm going to have to take the long way to your new home."

Andrew had read Hope's file three times and

studied the high-profile trial she'd testified in. He
was very familiar with the case that had made her
eligible for the program. However, it seemed as
if she knew more about the place she was b...
relocated to than he did.

"From what I read, this town was an admi-
lot of community spirit." ....
tone of her words.ig to find something positive
little too hard ...ng
rable situation that could be quite traumatizing.
Hope had been ripped out of the world she'd
known from her home in New Mexico. She'd be
cut off from the support of friends and family.
Now she had to build a life in a new state not
knowing anyone.

Because her life would be permanently under
threat, Hope also had to sever all ties to her past
and abandon her old profession as a schoolteacher. Which, he knew, couldn't be easy.

As Andrew turned the steering wheel, a banging noise caused him to whip his head around
to stare out the windshield. He'd been moving at
a snail's pace through the busy downtown side
street, but a man had stepped in front of his car.

The guy hit the hood of Andrew's car and
waved his fist in the air mouthing words that
Andrew suspected were expletives.

Hope gasped and jerked her head back.

For one moment, he locked eyes with the man. He looked familiar, but Andrew couldn't place him. The stranger's gaze lingered as well, his eyes growing wide. Then he whirled around and was enveloped by the crowd. Andrew didn't know anyone who lived in Whitetail. The man must have just looked like someone he knew. Still, the moment had made him uneasy.

"That guy has some anger issues," said Hope. "For sure."

Once he turned off on a street where there were fewer people, the GPS redirected him. He wove through a residential part of town, then past an auto repair shop and an insurance office to park in front of a building that resembled a red barn. The storefront sign indicated this was a pizza place.

Even though there was a neon Open sign, only one other car was parked in the front lot. It was seven o'clock. Most everyone must be downtown at the art walk.

Hope ran her fingers through her honey-brown hair. "This is where I'll be living?"

"There's an apartment above the pizza parlor in the back. We will provide you with a stipend until you can find a job. Once you have your own funds, you are free to find a different place in the area."

Hope nodded. "I see." She smiled but it didn't quite reach her eyes.

He detected the note of anguish in her voice.

She'd been quiet for most of the drive. Reality about her situation must be sinking in.

She cleared her throat. "You know what I'm going to miss the most?" Her voice wavered.

"What?"

"My second-grade kids, their precious hearts and the rhythm of the school year. I won't ever be able to teach again." She broke down crying.

Andrew reached over and rubbed her upper back. "It's going to be okay."

He always said that when a witness fell apart, but he wasn't sure it was true. Hope had lost everything to put a bad man behind bars. Lincoln Kramer, the number two man in a drug-dealing operation known as the Queen Bee Cartel, had killed Hope's brother, Craig. Hope had gone to check on her brother just as Lincoln fled, gun in hand. She'd had enough savvy to hide before she, too, was seen and shot.

Hope Miller was a woman who had suffered many losses in a short span of time. Though the death of her brother had been through violence, he felt empathy for her. His wife had died in a car accident only three years after they were married. To a degree, he understood her grief.

Andrew grabbed a tissue from the packet he kept on the console and handed it to her.

She wiped her eyes. "I'm sorry. I didn't mean to lose it."

His throat grew tight, though he tried to keep his voice steady and be strong for her. "It's understandable." After driving around to the back of the pizza place, he clicked himself out of his seat belt. "Come on, I'll walk you to your door."

Hope got out of the car. He grabbed a manila envelope from the back seat and pulled a set of keys out of it. They walked up an exterior staircase.

While she stood on the landing, she turned to face him, looking at him with round brown eyes. "I guess this is it."

"Remember if you have any trouble…don't hesitate to get in touch. I'm your point of contact with the program." He was saying the things he always said to a witness, but something felt different. He wanted to assure her, to make her feel safe. He handed her the envelope. "Your ID, new birth certificate and some cash. There is a phone in there set up under your new name. It has my number in it already." He pointed down at an older-model compact car in the employee parking lot, then held up the keys he'd pulled from the envelope. "For your car and your apartment."

She took the envelope and pulled out the driver's license. "My new last name is Lansburg."

Witnesses usually kept their first name. Less of a chance they wouldn't answer to the new name.

He studied her for a long moment. He'd escorted dozens of witnesses in his time as a marshal, then moved on. Why did walking away this time feel wrong?

"Take care, Hope… Lansburg." He turned and headed down the stairs. When he looked up, she was still standing there, watching him. The look of longing on her face cut right through him.

Andrew got into his car. Before starting the engine, he said a prayer for Hope's safety, and that she would find some happiness in her new life.

A few blocks from Hope's new place, Andrew was caught up in mini traffic jam close to downtown when he realized why the man who had banged on his car looked familiar. The realization sent shock waves through him.

Jason Zimmerman was a hit man who had ratted out his drug boss and cohorts in exchange for being put in WITSEC. Andrew had only seen his photo in the profile, and Jason's appearance had changed since then. Andrew had gotten the flu and another marshal had ended up escorting Jason. But Whitetail was not where Zimmerman had been placed, not even close. The shock on Zimmerman's face when he stepped in front of the car was not because he recognized Andrew. It was because he saw Hope. Was she Zimmerman's target?

Too much of a coincidence that Jason was here. That could mean only one thing.

Hope was in danger from a trained assassin.

His muscles tensed as the cars in front of him came to a standstill. He'd get back to her place faster if he ran. Andrew pulled into a parking space, pushed open his door and burst up the street back toward the pizza parlor.

After twisting the key in the lock, Hope pushed open the door to her new living space. She took in the white walls and new furniture. What word would she use to describe it? Definitely not *cozy*. "Sterile," she said out loud. Maybe some quilts and a little color would make a difference.

Her shoulders slumped. Whom was she kidding? She doubted that this place or this town would ever feel like home. The losses were just too great. She had nothing left of her old life and her brother was dead. She was starting with nothing, no home, no community.

She touched her hand to her heart and prayed. "Oh God, help me make a life here and to find some happiness."

The only bright spot was how empathetic Andrew had been. A sadness had come over her as she watched him walk back to his car. There was something very likeable about his easy smile and the brightness in his eyes. He exuded a confidence even when he was a little anxious and ran his hands through his short brown hair.

She stepped deeper into the apartment, setting the envelope and keys Andrew had given her on a narrow table by the door. What the apartment lacked in personality it made up for in being pristine and clean. It looked as though the update and remodel had been recent. The only thing not generic about it was that it smelled faintly like pepperoni.

The beige kitchen countertops looked new as did the stove. She moved to go check out the bedroom when the door swung open. Thinking it was Andrew come back to tell her something more, she pivoted as a hulk of a man filled the doorway, the man who had banged on the hood of Andrew's car.

Hope took a step back when she saw the gun in his hand. He grinned, revealing metal teeth.

"You're coming with me." His voice held the threat of violence.

Her breath caught and her heart pounded. She turned and ran for where the bedroom must be. The assailant leaped toward her, grabbing her shirttail and pulling her to him until he held a chunk of her hair.

Her head was bent back, and she could feel the gun press into her spine.

"You're hurting me."

Why was this happening? She was supposed to be safe here. He pushed her out on the landing, where the chatter of voices reached her ears. A tour bus had just pulled into the back lot and people were disembarking.

"I'm not going anywhere with you."

The man spoke under his breath leaning close to her ear. "Oh sure you are lady."

His proximity made her shudder.

When she glanced up the street, a man emerged from a side street running toward the pizza parlor. It was Andrew.

Hope took in a breath. He had come back to help her.

She stepped slightly to the side to block the assailant's view of Andrew. Once they were down the stairs, it wouldn't be so easy to spot him.

"Down the stairs now. And don't try anything," said the man with the metal teeth.

Only a few people from the tourist bus even glanced their way as she descended the stairs. Metal Teeth held the gun close to her body so it wouldn't be visible. If she cried out, would the man shoot her on the spot? It wasn't a chance she could take.

As the last tourist rounded the corner to get to the front of the pizza parlor, she saw the car that must belong to Metal Teeth. She couldn't see Andrew anywhere. What had happened? At the pace he'd been running, he had to be close.

The man pushed her toward the car. "Open the door, you're driving."

Hope reached for the door handle.

The man glanced side to side. She got in the car. The keys were not in the ignition. No chance of escaping by driving away.

Metal Teeth came around to the passenger side of the car and got in. He pulled the keys from his shirt pocket. "Drive to the marina."

"I don't know where that is," she said.

He still pointed the gun at her. "Get on Huffington Street." He tilted his head to indicate which road he meant. "Four blocks and take a right onto Windsor. Keep driving. You'll see the marina within minutes."

This man had clearly shown up with a plan. "Did someone from the Queen Bee Cartel send you? Is this revenge for my testimony against Lincoln Kramer?"

"I don't know nothing, lady. I just do my job and pick up my pay."

The street they were on had no other traffic as they drove by homes that looked largely unoccupied. Most everyone must be at the art walk.

"Turn up here," Metal Teeth commanded.

She hit her blinker just as she saw the street sign that indicated Windsor Street. Within minutes, she had a view of the marina. There were a few cars in front of her headed in the same direction. A Jeep without a roof slipped in behind them.

She checked the rearview mirror with a quick glance. There was a woman wearing a scarf in the Jeep.

What had happened to Andrew?

She had a sinking feeling she was driving to her death.

TWO

Once he saw that a man was leading Hope toward a car, Andrew knew he'd need a vehicle for pursuit. He couldn't get to her before that to pull his gun and stop the man. There was too much of a risk anyway that Jason would simply use Hope as a shield or just shoot her on the spot. Jason Zimmerman was a man without a conscience.

Andrew spotted a scooter with a helmet parked on the side of the pizza parlor. It must be used for deliveries. The key was in the ignition. He got on and turned the key. It sputtered to life. He put on the helmet and rolled forward toward the back parking lot just in time to see the car pull out onto the street. He'd make sure the scooter got back to its owner.

He followed the car, hanging back as it turned onto Windsor. When a Jeep made the same turn, he got on the street as well, but not for long. It was obvious Zimmerman was heading toward the marina.

Sharon Dunn

Heart pounding, he slipped onto a side street that ran parallel to Windsor, hoping he could beat the assassin to the marina. At first when he arrived at the marina, he did not see the car that Hope had been taken in. He parked the scooter and scanned the parking lot and then the dock. ~~attention~~ they gone?

much territory as he ~~continued~~ him to cover as at a pace that wouldn't call nondescript black compact, and ran toward it. His gun was concealed beneath his unzipped jacket in a shoulder holster. He unclicked the holster's leather strap as he approached the car. No one was in it.

The hit man must have already taken Hope onto one of the boats. He drew closer to the dock, running past each boat and listening for the sound of an engine starting up. The clatter and spin of a motor at the end of the pier caught his attention.

A midsized boat had pulled out into the water. The signage on its side indicated that it was one that was rented out. Zimmerman had known Hope's new address and had probably planned the abduction and later execution. It made sense that he would have rented a boat ahead of time. Some clear planning and insider knowledge had been a part of this crime. The insider knowledge element was the most disturbing. Only a limited number of people at Witness Protection and the marshals' office would know the exact location where witnesses were placed. The computer systems they used were extremely secure, but most a skilled outsider had found a way in the helm

Andrew ran to the dock where pulled out. He could see like Zimmerman, the from the back dark shoulder-length hair. The boat same had a below-deck area where Hope could be hidden. He stared at the long line of boats of varied sizes. Or she could be in one of the vessels that had remained in dock.

He took an educated guess and assumed that the hit man wanted to take her somewhere remote where there were no witnesses.

He sprinted along the dock until he saw a man in a motorboat with a sputtering engine. He pulled his ID and showed it to the man. "US marshal. I need this for official business."

The other boat was already arcing toward a curve in the lake and would soon be out of view.

"It's yours," the man said.

Andrew jumped in, squeezed the throttle and headed toward where he'd seen the other boat go. His small craft bumped over the waves. Once he rounded the forested shoreline where the rental boat had been headed, he encountered several other craft of different sizes.

From what he saw, Elk Horn Lake was huge with a thousand inlets and tributaries that were secluded. The lake narrowed as he went by several small forested islands. He passed a small ferry filled with passengers. Scanning the water as well as the islands, he did not see any sign of Zimmerman's rented boat. The hit man had to be heading somewhere there were no people, but Andrew could only guess at where that might be as he was faced with the option of turning east or south on the lake.

He did a wide circle. When he glanced south, he saw several boats, one that was playing loud music. However, in the part of the lake that veered east, he didn't spot any boats. He chose to go east. The lake opened up as the shoreline grew farther away. He passed only one small boat, a man holding a fishing pole sitting in it.

This part of the lake was so expansive that he could discern only one side of the shore, which he stayed close to. There was no secluded spot out here where a boat could go unnoticed.

He recalled from Jason Zimmerman's file that his method of assignation was usually a bullet to the head and then the body was tossed in the water. Not everyone who joined WITSEC was an innocent victim. Zimmerman had had such valuable information that it had been a trade-off to put him in witness protection with the promise that he would go straight in order to nab the people who pulled the strings for a huge part of the drug trade.

The wakes that pummeled his little craft indicated that a boat had recently traveled over this area. He prayed that it was the boat he was looking for. When he saw a narrow corridor off to the side, he made a guess that that was where Jason's boat had gone.

On this part of the lake, he could see two shorelines again. His boat cut through the waves, bumping and catching air when a stronger one hit his small craft. Another wake came toward him. A boat had definitely recently passed this way, and he hoped that he was chasing the right one.

He said a prayer that he'd made a solid spilt-second choice and that he would find Hope before it was too late.

The chugging of the boat motor was loud below deck, where Hope had been forced to go. She was grateful that the man who had kidnapped her had been in such a hurry that he'd not taken the time to tie her up.

When she pushed on the hatch that opened to above deck, it did not budge. Either a weight had been placed on it or it latched on the outside. In any case, it was the only route of escape.

Sooner or later, the man would have to stop for the purpose of killing her, she assumed. The thought sent chills through her body. Once that latch opened up, she had to be ready to escape. There must be something she could use as a weapon. Though it was dark and hard to see, she scooted around the tiny area looking for anything that might aid in a surprise attack. The ceiling was so low that she had to bend over to move around.

As she searched the cabinets, she found gas cans, water jugs, flares and a bucket of emergency food supply along with what looked like engine parts. She opened a dark cupboard and felt around. Her hand touched metal, a wrench.

Though it might be effective in fighting off someone, it was too big to hide in her pocket or waistband. If she held it behind her back, the kidnapper would be suspicious.

She set the wrench down and continued to search. After several minutes, she still had not found anything that would be helpful.

The engine grew quiet. She could hear the waves lapping against the hull of the boat. Her heart beat faster as heavy footsteps pounded above her. She was running out of time.

Then she saw her solution. A hook on the wall

close to the stairs that led above deck. She picked up the wrench and hung it there. She would be able to grab the weapon just as she emerged from below.

The footsteps drew closer, and she took a few steps back. The trapdoor was lifted, and light flooded below deck.

"Come on out, sweetheart, nice and slow," said her abductor.

She shaded her eyes from the evening sun. The intense light marred her view. She could only see the man's feet. He stood very close to the opening that led below deck. She stepped forward. Her foot rested on the first stair. The assailant took a step back. She still couldn't see his face, only his lower half. Her shoe touched the second step. As she put her foot on the third step, she reached toward where she had stashed the wrench. Her hands grasped metal.

"Hurry up," Metal Teeth barked.

She kept the hand holding the wrench low and to the side so the man would not notice it until the last second. The final step would put her above deck. In one swift motion, she jumped up and started swinging.

Caught by surprise, her kidnapper stumbled backward. He raised the gun to shoot her just as she landed a blow to his chest and then she hit the arm that held the weapon. He groaned in pain and dropped it.

She swung at him again, but he angled to one side and dodged the blow. He lunged toward her, forcing her to step backward. She dared not look behind her to determine where the open hatch was. She had to guess and pray she didn't fall below deck.

The man continued to advance toward her, "You think you can outfight me? You got another thing coming."

She held the wrench up, ready to swing when he got close.

"Try it lady." He grinned and narrowed his eyes. "Just try it."

The boat listed to one side. They both stumbled. She landed on one knee but scrambled to get back on her feet. The man fell on his side.

The gun slid across the deck toward the boat's edge.

The assailant crawled toward it just as it fell into the water. He groaned and cursed. Metal Teeth was still on his knees.

While he was vulnerable, Hope stepped toward him.

He was halfway to a standing position just as she got close enough to hit him in the leg. The man groaned in pain but kept trying to get to his feet.

The boat swayed again, and she fell on all fours, bracing herself with her hands. She'd let go of the wrench but grabbed it before it slid toward the assailant when the boat rocked again.

The man had time to burst to his feet and come at her before she could push herself to a standing position.

When he got close enough, she swung the wrench, stopping him only a few feet from her. The move gave her time to get to her feet while she kept her eyes on the man who intended to kill her.

As she was still finding her balance on the wobbling boat, he charged toward her. He grabbed her free hand at the wrist. She hit him with the wrench in the shoulder, but her swing was weak.

He secured her other wrist. "Drop the wrench."

Her attacker forced her back so that her spine pressed against the railing. He squeezed her nerve endings in her wrist, causing intense pain. She dropped the wrench. It fell on his foot, but the heavy boots he wore probably protected him from pain as he continued to push her into the railing.

His face was so close to hers she could feel his breath on her cheek.

"Please, you're hurting me," she whimpered.

His eyes had a wild quality that scared her. Her

cries of pain produced not a flicker of empathy in his expression.

She lifted her knee and slammed it between his legs. He let go of her, lurched back and bent over.

It was now or never.

She turned, put her foot on the railing and swung her leg over, plunging into the water. Waves hit her and pulled her under before she could start swimming. She resurfaced, slicing her arms through the water. The shore was visible but far away. Thankfully, the boat was big enough that it wouldn't be able to follow her into the shallow water if he chose to try to catch her that way.

As she swam, she waited for the sound of an engine starting up but heard only the waves lapping around her.

When she dared to glance over her shoulder, she saw that the man had inflated a small lifeboat and was paddling toward her.

Her arms and legs grew fatigued as the man closed the distance between them. She kept her eyes on the rocky beach up ahead. After all she had been through and lost, she was not about to let this man kill her. Justice had to prevail. The thought made her swim faster. Water splashed around her as her arms cut through the current.

"Not so fast."

A hand grabbed her hair and pulled her backward. Her shoulder brushed the side of the lifeboat, and she was dragged into it. Out of breath, Hope crawled away from Metal Teeth. He grasped her feet and dragged her toward him.

She saw the wrench lying in the lifeboat and watched in horror as his fingers circled around the handle while his other hand held on to her by her shirt.

"Where did you put your brother's things?"

The question was so out of the blue, she could barely process it. "What are you talking about?"

Suddenly, she felt an odd sensation impacting the back of her head. Her vision filled with tiny black dots until darkness overtook her. The last sound she heard was the waves hitting the boat....

When she came to, they were back on the larger boat. Her hands and feet were tied, and her feet had been weighted down with motor parts and the wrench.

Metal Teeth kneeled down and grabbed her chin, squeezing both sides of her face. "Tell me where your brother's stuff is, and I'll let you go."

She looked into his eyes. He was lying. No matter what, he was going to kill her.

THREE

Andrew's breath caught when he saw the boat up ahead. Jason Zimmerman was standing on deck, holding Hope by the back of her collar. Her hands and feet were bound and her feet appeared to have weights attached. They stood at the back of the boat where there was no railing.

Zimmerman locked eyes with Andrew, then pushed Hope into the water. As the splash of impact faded, the hit man ran toward the helm of the boat. The engine roared to life and the larger craft sped away.

When Andrew got to the spot where Hope had been pushed, he dived into the water. His hands found her arm, but the weights tied to her body meant it would take a Herculean effort to pull her to the surface.

He tried swimming upward with just one arm but made no progress. Desperation clawing through him, he worked his way down, holding on to her until he could see the ropes that held the weight. Knowing that he could not hold his breath for long, he pulled a pocketknife out and cut the rope. Hope started to rise to the surface. She moved her bound feet in an effort to swim. He held on to her as he burst above the water, gasping for air. One more second and he could have passed out.

Andrew pulled Hope up, so her head was above the waves. They both bobbed on the surface. He held on to her so she wouldn't sink. With her legs and hands still tied up, swimming would be impossible. He glanced around. Jason Zimmerman had been in such a hurry that he left the lifeboat behind. With some effort, he swam toward it, got in himself and dragged Hope in as well.

He put his face close to hers. "You okay?"

She stared at him with glazed eyes as water drained off her face. The shock of nearly dying had not yet worn off, but she managed a nod. "If you hadn't come when you did, I would have drowned."

Water dripped off both of them, splatting on the floor of the lifeboat. He pressed his hand against her smooth cheek, hoping his touch would keep her from going deeper into shock. "All in a day's work."

After cutting the ropes around her wrists and ankles, he paddled back toward where his borrowed motorboat was.

Hope seemed to be more alert as she wrung the water out of her hair and then twisted her shirt hem to do the same.

Though it was a warm summer day, they both were shivering from having been in the water. He paddled until they were lined up with the motorboat. He crawled in and then turned holding a hand out to her. "Let me help you."

She took his hand and lifted her leg to transfer from one boat to the other. They were face to face. She looked into his eyes. "Thank you."

As he settled into the boat, he wondered if it would even be safe to go back to Whitetail since it was clear that location was compromised.

He craned his neck to see if she was sitting down. "Ready?"

She nodded.

Hope was going to have to start the relocation process all over again, but there would be no point to doing that until the source of the leaked information was found. He still hoped that someone from the outside had hacked into the system and discovered the information, a much easier problem to deal with than rooting out who in the organization was corrupt. He didn't have a clue who it could be at this point.

"Where are we going?" Her voice was still weak.

"Not sure just yet." He needed time to think

through what his next move should be. "How about we find a place where we can get warmed up and dried off?"

He scooted forward on the seat, yanked the pull cord on the motor. It revved to life.

She wrapped her arms around her body and stared at the bottom of the boat. She looked so vulnerable.

"Hang in there." He sped forward through the water.

When he glanced back, Hope had turned her head and looked over her shoulder in the direction the assassin had escaped to.

Up ahead, two other boats had come into the secluded inlet.

He decided it wouldn't be a good idea to go back to the marina. The hit man had to return the boat he'd rented. Also, Andrew wondered if Zimmerman would wait around for news of a body being found. Often hit men did not get paid until they could show proof that they had accomplished the deed. Jason Zimmerman had sped away because he didn't want to be caught. He probably didn't realize that Andrew could identify him.

He bumped over the waves and skimmed the smoother parts of the water. He saw a sign for the Lakeside Inn and Restaurant and pulled into the dock where several other boats were parked.

The inn consisted of a two-story building that looked like it belonged on Cape Cod, not in Montana. They'd be able to get dried off here, and he could call someone he trusted. Bryson Whitman was the head of the marshals for the New Mexico District, where Hope was from, and Andrew's direct supervisor. He was leery of communicating with the administrative part of WITSEC if that was where security had been breached and put Hope's life in danger. It was possible that the leak about Hope's location had happened with the marshals as well. He wasn't sure who would have access to the info on Hope. WITSEC had a case manager for each witness, but who else had access to that information?

They both got out of the boat and headed up the dock toward the inn. Two cars were parked in the lot.

Hope grabbed his hand. "He came back."

Andrew turned to face her. "What?"

"The man who tried to kill me. He brought his boat back around. I saw him just as we went around a bend when I looked over my shoulder. I was too much in shock to say anything."

"Probably coming back to see if he succeeded in his mission," Andrew told her. "Did he see us?"

She shook her head. "Not sure."

There had been other boats in the inlet by then.

The hit man didn't want witnesses so he wouldn't have come after them again if he had seen them. It was also a possibility that Jason had turned around to head back to the marina.

"That means we can't stay here long," Andrew said.

His shoes squished with each step. They both looked like they'd gone swimming fully clothed. His wallet was secure inside a zippered pocket of his jacket, but he was pretty sure his phone was toast. In diving into the water, he'd lost his gun. He'd left the leather strap disconnected.

When they got inside, Andrew opted to tell the truth but gave the edited version as to why two adults in street clothes were soaking wet. "We fell in the water."

The front desk clerk only stared at them for a few seconds before checking to see which room was available. She set a key on the counter. "Room twelve at the back. Dinner is between five and nine. Snacks available after that. The pool closes at ten."

Next to check-in was a small gift shop. Andrew grabbed two T-shirts with the inn logo on them as well as two pairs of board shorts. He paid for them. "I don't suppose that there's a laundry in this place."

"If you leave your wet clothes outside the door, I'll grab them and throw them in with the linens and towels," the clerk said. "I can get them to you in a couple of hours. I was about to run a load anyway."

Room twelve was on the second floor and had no view of the lake but looked down on the pool area. Fine by him, he wasn't here as a tourist. He handed Hope the smaller T-shirt and shorts. At least the color had come back into her cheeks. "Why don't you get dried off first?"

"All right…thanks." She took the clothes and headed toward the bathroom. A second later, he heard the shower running.

Andrew picked up the hotel phone to talk to his direct supervisor on his personal cell. It was after the time people would be at the office. But even if it had been office hours, he would not have used the marshals' office phone. If a breach had occurred, the phone might be bugged.

Bryson Whitman picked up after the third ring. "Hello?"

"Bryson, it's Andrew. We've had a serious complication with the placement of Hope Miller. Jason Zimmerman came after her."

"Zimmerman? Wasn't his placement in Washington State? Looks like he just couldn't leave his old life behind," Bryson said.

"It gets worse. He knew the address of where she'd be living. Somewhere down the line, the placement was leaked and compromised, and they pulled an assassin from the program," Andrew told him. "I don't want it to be true, but all of this screams inside job to me."

"Only a few people in WITSEC would have authorized access to her file," his supervisor said.

"Maybe someone not authorized got a peek at it. So the question I'm asking is how hackable is that information from the inside or the outside? Or maybe someone just looked over someone's shoulder or knew them well enough to guess at the passwords. I can't turn Hope back over to WITSEC until I know she'll be safe."

"Let me do some discreet poking around and see what I can figure out," Bryson said.

"You'll have no way to reach me. My phone got ruined by the water. Even if I did have it, I think I would ditch it for something more disposable anyway."

"Give me a day or so and then you get in touch with me in a way that you deem is secure," his boss suggested.

"Okay. And in the meantime, I'm going to have to stay close to Hope." Andrew blew out a breath. "Zimmerman tried to drown her, but I am concerned he will figure out I got to her in time."

"Stay safe. I'll let you know what I find out," Bryson said.

Andrew hung up. He stared out the window for a long moment. He was on his own in protecting Hope for now. The potential for her to die brought back his grief over the loss of his wife as though it were brand-new. He vowed that Hope would not be killed on his watch.

Hope emerged from the bathroom wearing the brightly colored board shorts and T-shirt and holding her wet clothes. He rose to his feet, grabbing the dry clothes he'd bought for himself.

Her eyes searched his. "What is going to happen to me now?" Her voice lilted as she spoke.

"Obviously, you will need a new placement and identity. There's just going to be a little bit of a delay." He detected the fear behind her words and how she was looking to him for help and guidance. He'd do everything in his power to keep her safe.

"I suppose it takes time to create a whole new person," she murmured.

She had been through enough trauma for a lifetime. He didn't want to burden her with his concern that there was a leak in the program. "I'll stay with you until we can get you a new and more secure placement."

"He's going to come for me again, isn't he? That man with the metal teeth."

"Maybe, if he figures out he didn't finish the job. I know who he is, by the way. His name is Jason Zimmerman."

Her eyes widened. "How do you know his name?"

"Let's just say we crossed paths as part of my job." Again, it felt like giving her fewer details would ease the fear he saw etched on her beautiful face.

"He's dangerous." A chill came into her voice. "His eyes were dead."

Andrew nodded. "We just need to hang low until we can get this all sorted out."

"Okay." Hope sat down on the end of the bed.

Before retreating to the bathroom to get dried off and changed, he drew the curtains shut and turned the deadbolt. If the assassin did stop at the inn and spotted her through the window, she'd be an easy target.

The thought of harm coming to her again caused a tightness in his chest. "Stay away from the window out of sight."

"I will." She nodded. She pressed her lips together as her forehead wrinkled and her voice held a note of angst.

Hope could hear the shower running in the bathroom as she turned on the television and clicked through several channels before turning it off. She burst up from the bed and paced. She didn't even have the focus to pay attention to a mindless television program.

She'd been cut off from everyone in her life in New Mexico. And now the new identity she'd been given was ripped from her in the blink of an eye. The few possessions she'd been allowed to take with her were back in the one-bedroom apartment that smelled like pepperoni. She would probably not be able to retrieve them. How much more would be taken from her?

Her only sense of stability was Andrew. He was the one thing that linked her back to her old life.

She stopped herself before her thoughts spiraled out of control. She knew, too, that no matter what, God was with her. That truth kept her from giving in to despair.

She caught a glimpse of herself in the mirror on the dresser. She didn't even look like Hope Miller. Her long blond hair had been dyed light brown and cut shorter, barely touching her shoulders.

Feeling numb, she sat down at the end of the bed and stared at the wall. She was not aware of how much time had passed when Andrew emerged from the bathroom in his dry clothes.

He placed the wet towels and clothes outside the door, then drew the curtain back a few inches and peered out. He turned back to face her. "I'm starving. Why don't we go grab something to eat."

"Sure." The clock on the nightstand indicated they could still make dinner.

As they moved through the hallway and down the stairs, Andrew remained close to her. Both of them were keenly aware at how fragile their situation was. Jason Zimmerman might still be looking for her or waiting around to hear a report of her death.

Only Andrew's proximity quelled her fear as his shoulder brushed against hers.

The dining room was small, four tables and a counter.

"Let's get something that's quick," Andrew said. "We can eat back in the room."

It was clear being out in the open was not a good idea. If he had seen their boat, would the assassin return to the marina in Whitetail first to look for her and then backtrack? Or would he check the places along the shoreline for them?

They both grabbed a menu while they stood at the counter. There was no one eating in the dining room, and she didn't see any sign of a waitress. Laughter, conversation and the noise of pots being banged around spilled out from behind the swinging doors of the kitchen.

She stared at the menu. "I have an odd craving for pepperoni pizza."

Andrew laughed at her joke. The moment of

levity eased some of the tension in her body. She was glad she could make him laugh.

A teenage boy emerged from the kitchen. "Hey, eating late, huh? What can I get you?"

"We'd like something we could take back to our room."

"Mom always puts together some premade sandwiches and salads." He angled his body toward the kitchen doors as if that would help him remember. "I think we got a Cobb salad left and a couple of BLTs, or we have chili you can heat up in the microwave in your room. Comes with a corn bread muffin."

Andrew looked at Hope.

"The chili sounds good," she said.

"I'll have the same. Toss in one of those sandwiches for me as well," Andrew told him.

The teenager slipped behind the swinging doors and returned a few minutes later with a brown paper bag. "Napkins and utensils are over by the door."

After paying, Andrew carried the bag while Hope grabbed several napkins and packages of plastic utensils.

They stepped outside where she had a view of the office check-in area, which had glass doors. Her breath caught and she took a step back. "It's him." Even from the back she recognized the dark hair and muscular build of the man who had tried to kill her.

Andrew drew his attention to where she was looking just as Jason was about to turn. He pulled Hope behind a stack of kayaks.

The assassin walked by, his footsteps heavy on the sidewalk. He was headed toward the entrance that would lead to room twelve. If they hadn't been out getting food, they would have been easy targets.

Andrew pressed close to her and whispered in her ear, "We have to get out of here."

He placed the food on the ground and ushered her out into the open. They had only minutes until the assassin would realize they were not in their room.

They hurried toward the dock, passing the rental boat Jason had used. The ferry that advertised lake tours was docked at the end of the pier. Several people boarded.

When she glanced over her shoulder, she didn't see the hit man anywhere. Would he break the door down and search the room or just go looking for them on the grounds? The desk clerk must have revealed that a couple matching their description had checked in. She could only guess at what kind of story Jason had told to get the information. In any case, they didn't have long to find a hiding place.

"Being with people is the safest," Andrew said. He approached the man standing at the end of the plank that connected to the dock by the ferry. "How much for a tour?"

"Tour's half over. Most people board at Whitetail, which is where we are headed next after watching the sunset."

Andrew stretched his arm across Hope's back and drew her close. "We're just looking for something fun to do for the evening."

The warmth of his touch soaked through her skin and calmed her.

The man shrugged. "We dock for the night at Whitetail. You'll have to find your own ride back to the inn if that's where you're staying."

"That's sounds good." He nudged Hope forward. "We'll pay for the whole tour. You can run my credit card once we're on board."

"Sure, whatever."

The engine of the vessel had already starting humming. Andrew and Hope slipped inside the below-deck area of the boat as the man pulled in the plank.

The lower-deck area had seating that circled all the way around and small round windows to look out of. Besides an older couple, they were the only ones in the space as the boat pulled back out into the water.

Hope peered out the window. The assassin was

making his way down the dock. She slipped back on the seat cushion to be out of view as her heart pounded.

Andrew sat close to her. He ran his hands through his neatly cut brown hair. He was on edge, too.

The older man wrapped his arm around the older woman. "Looks like we're the only ones not enjoying the sunset. Mary got a little seasick."

"Guess I'm just a landlubber," Mary said.

The boat gained speed as waves sloshed against the hull.

"Sunsets on the lake are supposed to be quite wonderful," the older gentleman remarked. "You two should head on up and enjoy yourselves."

"Maybe in a bit," Andrew replied. "We've had kind of a long day. It's nice to be someplace quiet."

The sweetness of the interaction between the older husband and wife touched her heart and made her smile. Would she ever experience anything like that now that her life was permanently under threat?

"You've got a little time anyway. Mary and I might head up if she's feeling up to it." He patted his wife's arm.

The tone of his voice suggested that Andrew had no intention of going out where they might be spotted. If the assassin didn't find them around the inn, he'd assume they'd left on a boat and start looking for them on the lake.

Though the ferry provided a brief reprieve, they were far from safe.

FOUR

Andrew was grateful that Hope felt comfortable enough with him to rest her head on his shoulder. The sound of her breathing indicated she'd fallen asleep. The intensity of all she had been through had obviously caught up with her.

It felt good to have her close, but it bothered him that such a violent event had led to her exhaustion. He felt his resolve to keep her safe harden.

Though he was fatigued, too, his mind raced too fast for him to even close his eyes.

The older couple had opted to try going above deck, so they were alone except for the occasional passenger who came below to use the restroom.

Footsteps and laughter resounded above him. He felt far removed from the frivolity of a tourist enjoying a summer evening. The boat stopped for about twenty minutes. People must be watching the sunset.

Andrew remained still so Hope could rest. In spite of all that was on his mind, he found himself relaxing a little as he listened to the steady rhythm of her breathing.

Once the boat started up again, the man who had greeted them when they boarded came below deck. "Well, that's the end of the tour. We're almost to the marina. I don't think I ever saw you on deck."

"Guess we were more tired than we realized," Andrew murmured.

Hope stirred awake and lifted her head. A faint smile graced her face when she looked at him.

Her expression warmed his heart. "Glad you could get some sleep." He turned his attention back to the man who had let them on the boat. "I never did pay you for the ride," he said.

The man waved the idea away with his hand. "Don't worry about it. The cruise wasn't full anyway. You folks enjoy your evening. We should be docking in about five minutes."

Once the man left, Andrew turned to look at Hope. "You ready?"

She nodded. "Do you have a plan? Is someone from WITSEC going to come for me? How does this work?" Her voice faltered.

She was looking to him for help. She had no one else. He felt the weight of that responsibility.

The boat slowed as the motor made grinding noises and then it came to a full stop.

He'd have to explain his suspicions to her sooner or later. But since she already had so much to deal with, the short version of why he wasn't contacting WITSEC felt like the best option. "Not just yet. I'm waiting to hear from my direct supervisor. Once I talk to him, maybe we can come up with a long-term plan for you. We need to find a place to hide out for the night."

"Hide out?" she asked. "Help is not coming tonight?"

He'd do anything to make her less afraid. "I'll get this straightened out as fast as I can. I promise, Hope. I just want to assure you, you're in safe hands as long as you're with me. Remember that."

Though her expression indicated she was upset, she nodded.

They moved to the above-deck area and disembarked.

Hope gazed back at the boat once they were on land. "It looks so pretty with those lights strung around the railing. Viewing the sunset from there must have been spectacular." Her voice filled with longing.

So much had been taken from her. It was such a small thing to be able to view a beautiful sunset, but she had even been robbed of the possibility. "Maybe someday you will get a chance to do something fun like that."

The parking lot at the marina was less full than it had been earlier. Andrew spotted a rental boat that was the same model as the one the assassin had been on. He was sure there were plenty of other rental boats, but he couldn't take any chances.

"Let's try to stay out of sight as much as possible." He ushered her behind a closed coffee hut. Though it was not that far back into town, walking and being out in the open was out of the question. He'd noticed several taxis in the area and wondered if it would be safe to hail one.

If they could get back into town, they could get to his car. It was a risk all the same. Zimmerman had seen what kind of car he drove and might have been able to locate it and was waiting for their return.

He peered out and watched for a taxi. More cars pulled out of the lot as boats docked for the evening.

"We're going back into Whitetail?" Her voice held a note of fear.

"Just to get the car where I left it," Andrew answered. "It's the only way to get out of here quickly."

A taxi showed up at the edge of the lot. He stepped out and waved the car over while he surveyed the area around him. It was dark enough that he could not see people clearly as they walked through the lot. That meant folks couldn't see them, either.

They got into the taxi and Andrew instructed the driver. "My car is on the street just off of Main by a hardware store."

"I know which one you are talking about," the driver replied.

The driver rolled away from the marina back into town. Main Street looked almost abandoned at this time of night, a sharp contrast from hours before when the streets had been filled with people enjoying the art walk. The barriers that kept traffic off Main Street had been taken down. Most the shop windows were dark except for a few restaurants and bars.

The driver pulled in behind Andrew's car. They got out, and he paid the driver. His keys had been in the same zippered pocket as his wallet.

Though a few people were wandering Main Street, there was no one on this side street. He studied the shadowed areas underneath the eaves and up the ally before getting in the car.

Hope got into the passenger seat.

He pulled out onto the street and headed toward the edge of town.

She turned to look through the rear windshield. "That seemed like a nice little town. Maybe I could have learned to be happy there."

"We'll find you a place to live, a safe place," he assured her.

"My parents died years ago, so after Craig was killed, I really had no immediate relatives. I thought I would be okay becoming someone different in a new place. And I wanted justice for my brother's death."

"Now you're not so sure?"

"I left behind lots of friends and years of being a part of a community." She shook her head and ran her fingers through her hair. "I just thought I would be settling into a quiet, anonymous life. This has been way more excitement than I needed for a lifetime. Of course, maybe you like the excitement."

"I don't like you being in danger, but yes, one of the reasons I like my job is the adrenaline rush." He thought, too, that maybe after his wife had died, pouring himself into the action of his job had numbed the pain. If he shared that with her, would she understand?

"I'd take my old boring life anytime," she murmured.

"Hopefully, we can give you that."

They passed the first sign that listed the next towns. Longview was only twenty miles down the road. He had no idea how big the town was or what he would find there. All they needed for now was a safe place to wait out the night and somewhere to get a phone so he could get in touch with Bryson.

For the next few miles, they encountered only one car headed in the other direction. Suddenly, his car engine made a stuttering noise. Andrew shifted down. Something was wrong with the engine. By the time he pulled over on the shoulder, the noise had intensified to a metallic clacking sound.

"What's wrong?" she asked.

"Not sure. But I'm going to go see what the problem is."

Andrew turned the car off, pressed the button that opened the hood and got out. He flung open the hood and leaned in trying to see in the dark. The burnt smell was not a good sign.

Hope stood beside him. "I found this in the glove compartment." She turned the flashlight on and shined it on the engine.

It looked like the timing belt had torn and come off.

Andrew had not had time to lock his car when he'd run to save Hope. It was possible that this was not a breakdown but sabotage. Something designed to get them a few miles outside of town away from people before they broke down.

"Shine the light right here." He pointed toward the broken belt. It could have been cut to the point that it would break after a short drive.

Hope stepped a few feet away from the car, so she had a view of the road. "Here comes a car. Maybe the driver can give us a ride."

Adrenaline surged through Andrew. "Hope, get on the passenger side of the car away from the road and stay down." His voice became urgent. "That might not be help at all."

It might be the assassin coming to finish them off.

Hope pressed her hand against the cold metal of the car. Andrew positioned himself in front of her.

Her heart beat faster at the sound of the other car pulling off the road as tires crunched on the gravel. She winced when the headlights of the other car flooded the area.

Andrew lifted his head, probably trying to see the driver without being seen himself.

For what felt like an eternity, she listened to the other car's engine hum while the headlights remained on. Why hadn't the driver gotten out to see if they needed help?

Andrew turned and spoke in a low voice. "Go to the front of the car, stay low and run away from the road. I'll be right behind you."

He must have seen something that indicated the man in the car was the assassin.

By the time she made it to the front bumper, she heard a car door slam.

Hope sprinted across what appeared to be a meadow. It was so dark that what lay ahead was only shadows. Though she held the flashlight, she dare not turn it on and give herself away. She heard Andrew's footsteps behind her, making a swishing noise as he moved through the tall grass.

The hit man had lost his gun on the boat. Unless he had found time to acquire another one, he was unarmed.

A mechanical hum reached her ears just as headlights flooded the area. The man had decided to use his car as a weapon. He was driving across the field after them.

Fear for her life caused her to run even faster.

Andrew pulled on her sleeve as they veered away from the car headlights and into the darkness.

The grinding of gears and the car shifting into Reverse indicated that the man was trying to re-orient in the direction they had turned.

She almost slammed into the fence before she saw it. Her hand touched the dry wood of a fence pole.

When she glanced over her shoulder, the headlights were headed toward them but at a much slower pace. The terrain was rougher, not something that was meant to be driven on.

"Climb over," Andrew commanded.

After putting the flashlight in her pocket, she fumbled to find the lower horizontal fence railing and flung her leg over the top rail. Andrew had already jumped over. He reached up to help her down, so she landed on her feet.

They kept running. The car stopped at the fence. The headlights were turned off. They were so far from any dwelling or artificial light that darkness engulfed them.

She turned her ears to the sound of the assassin coming after them. A thudding noise behind her could be him. What was he planning on doing? He had no gun and there were two of them. She did remember seeing a knife sheath around his belt. If Jason had been sent to kill her, he probably had more than one way to do that.

The notion of dying from a knife wound gave her the incentive to keep running.

They sprinted until they were both gasping for air. When they slowed to a jog, she was able to hear better. If the man was still behind them, he was being very quiet.

"Do you think he gave up?" She took a breath between each word.

"Not sure." Andrew stopped.

They waited for several minutes, not hearing or seeing anything that indicated they were still being followed.

"Do you think it's okay if I turn on the flashlight to see what is around here?"

"For a quick second," Andrew told her.

She pulled the flashlight out of her pocket, turned and clicked it on, swinging it in an arc.

The light did not reach very far, but she could see nothing but the tall grass they'd just come through. No sign of the assailant. Maybe he'd given up.

Hope turned and shined the light in the other direction. With the small area that the light illuminated, all she could see was open field. No lights, no building, no road.

It was still hours before sunrise.

"Let's keep going." Andrew brushed her sleeve. "We're bound to run into something sooner or later."

She wasn't so sure about that.

Hope had only taken two steps when a force that felt like a brick wall slammed into her. She dropped the flashlight, which she'd turned off. Hands held her down at the wrists. Heavy breathing surrounded her and then she heard Andrew strike a blow against the assassin.

The noise of slaps and hits being landed pummeled her ears. The attacker groaned. One of the men cried out as if in pain, but she could not discern who. Hope rose to her feet and moved toward the fight.

She heard the cacophony of one man hitting another and then silence fell around her.

Andrew's hand found hers in the dark. "Let's go." Something about his voice sounded different, anguished.

She had no idea what had happened to the other man. Andrew tired quickly as they ran. His breathing intensified even though they slowed to a trot. She noticed that his hand rested across his stomach and he bent forward.

She cringed. "He cut you. Oh, Andrew…"

"It's nothing." He sounded like he was speaking through gritted teeth.

Maybe Andrew had subdued the other man or even killed him, but now they were miles from anything, and he had a knife wound that he'd gotten trying to protect her. More sacrifice on his part.

Up ahead, a cluster of aspen trees came into view. The white bark stood in contrast to the dark that surrounded them.

Andrew fell to the ground, resting his back against a tree trunk.

Hope sat down beside him. His breathing sounded raspy and forced. "How bad is the cut?"

"Not deep but long, I think. I just need a moment to catch my breath."

"The other man?"

"I knocked him out."

Would the assassin come looking for them once he came to or would he give up and return to his vehicle? They couldn't wait around here to find out.

Andrew needed medical attention. They had to find help or a way back to town. No way was she going to let him be in pain if she could help it.

She rose to her feet and held out her hand, trying to inject strength into her voice. "Come on, I'll help you walk."

He grasped her hand, and she pulled him to his feet. They'd run for miles. And the darkness disoriented her.

She wrapped her arm around his waist, and he flung his arm across her back and squeezed her shoulder.

"What is your best guess as to where the road might be?" she asked.

He turned his head. In every direction, there was nothing but grassy fields. The fence had been the only landmark they'd run into.

"Let's try this way," Andrew suggested.

They trudged through darkness.

As they walked, she found herself praying silently. That they were headed in the right direction. That they would find help.

Now as she listened to Andrew's breathing

grow more labored, it was clear he was not doing so well. She had no idea how much blood he'd lost. He was the kind of man who didn't want her to worry, so he might be underplaying how badly he was hurt.

He had taken risks to save her from the assassin. She had to find a way to help him.

More than anything, she prayed for a reprieve from being hunted down by the man with the metal teeth. It was clear they were in no shape for another encounter with him.

FIVE

Initially Andrew's hand had been soaked with blood. His shirt as well was wet around the area of the wound. The bleeding had stopped but the cut stung. And the blood loss made him weak.

"Hey, that looks like something over there." Hope pointed with her chin.

He lifted his head. It took a minute for a dark outline to come into view. A building, maybe, but no lights.

They kept walking. The ground beneath him changed from grass to an asphalt road that was in need of repair. They walked around the potholes and the places where the edges of the broken asphalt pushed together to create tiny mountains. The building was boarded up. A dusty sign lying on the ground indicated that it had once been a roadside café and gas station. An abandoned building was not what either of them had been hoping for.

"I'll see if there is a way in. Maybe there is something that will tell us where we are at least." She touched his shoulder. "You stay here."

He did not have the strength to argue with her. He leaned against an old gas pump. His injury seemed to have given her newfound strength. He was just grateful the assassin had not been able to kill her.

Judging from how deteriorated the road was, he doubted that anyone had been here in years. A new road must have been built elsewhere, making the gas station obsolete.

She yanked on the wood across the windows and doors but couldn't create an entryway. Hope disappeared around a corner.

She returned a few minutes later. "I found a way in. There's a place for you to at least sit down." She reached out for him and guided him around the corner. The plywood had been taken off a back door and laid to one side. She pushed the door open, and they entered what must have been a kitchen at one time. The grills had been torn out and cupboards lay on the floor.

"This way," she said. "I found a chair that is pretty sturdy."

She led him through the kitchen into the dining area past a counter that had broken glass and empty food cans on it.

She helped him sit in a padded chair. Even to

be able to finally stop moving eased his pain. "That's nice," he said.

"I'm going to see what I can find." She moved back into the kitchen. He could hear her opening cupboards and stepping over the debris-laden floor.

As his eyes adjusted to the darkness, he saw open cans and a sleeping bag on the floor. Someone must have squatted here at one time. That explained why the back door had been torn open.

Hope came back into the dining room and scoured the area behind the counter.

What was she hoping to find? A first aid kit? A map that explained where they were?

She approached him, her voice intensifying as she reached out toward him. "How are you doing?"

He sucked air through his teeth. "I'm all right. You keep looking around."

"You sure?"

"Yes." He was hurting but he didn't want to worry her.

Sighing, she walked past him through a wide arched doorway. The counter, the dilapidated cash register and the shelving indicated that that part of the building had probably been a convenience store.

She rummaged around for several minutes, disappearing from view. He closed his eyes, trying to keep his breathing shallow so he wouldn't feel the pain of the cut.

She returned holding a small piece of paper in her hand. "I know where this place is."

He shook his head. "How did you figure that out?"

She showed him the piece of paper, which was a torn and stained receipt. "This is Leman's Café. The Lemans were a prominent family in White-tail…a lot of the stores still have their name. It was in the guidebook I read. I can't help myself. I'm a teacher. I like learning new things."

"Don't apologize. Your curiosity about where you were going to be living may help us get back to civilization."

"There was a photo of this place in the article I read," she continued. "Obviously in better shape when it was still open in the eighties. Anyway, when they built the new four-lane road to the lake, this café closed."

He shook his head, still not understanding. "So what does that mean in terms of where we're at?"

"This café and gas station were used by every-one on their way to Elkhorn Lake. The pictures showed a campground next to it with a creek."

"Are you saying we can't be that far from the lake?"

She nodded. "It's the other side of the lake, not the part that connects with the town. I bet by morning when we can see more, we'll be able to figure out how to get back to the lake and people."

"Okay." Rest sounded good to him. "We should run into someone who can give us a ride."

"I found some plastic cups still in their packaging in there." She pointed toward the convenience store area. "Maybe that creek hasn't dried up. I can get us some water to drink."

The mention of water made him realize how thirsty and hungry he was. He had had to ditch their dinner back at the inn. "You shouldn't go alone." He leaned forward, and pain shot across his belly.

She patted his back. "Sit and rest. I'll just look around close to the building."

Her touch warmed his skin.

Before he could protest, she went into the kitchen area, where the open back door was.

His eyelids grew heavy with fatigue, and his head slumped forward. When he woke, he wasn't sure how much time had passed. Ten minutes. Or was it an hour? He called Hope's name but heard no reply. Had something happened to her? He kicked himself mentally for falling asleep.

With some effort, he pushed himself to his feet, bracing his hand on the back of the chair and wincing. He shuffled back into the kitchen toward the open door. It was still dark outside.

The bushes and small trees were so overgrown they came almost all the way up to the back door. Beyond that was old-growth forest. Wind rustled through the trees, but he did not hear anything else.

Feeling a rising panic, he took a step toward the forest. Was it possible the assassin had followed them here? He'd shown himself to be tenacious so far. He never should have let Hope be outside alone.

"Hope?" He stepped deeper into the forest as pain surged through him.

A rustling noise caused him to take shelter behind a tree. He peered out, not able to see much but shadows.

Hope emerged from the trees, her pale skin and lighter-colored hair easy to see against the darker shadows.

He said her name again.

She rushed toward him. "You're supposed to be resting."

"I got worried about you. How long has it been?"

"I don't know…half an hour. It took me a while to find the creek in the dark." She held two cups in her hand. "Here…drink. I've already had some."

He took the cup from her hand. The cool liquid felt wonderful on his parched throat. The water sloshed in his empty stomach. "That helps, thanks."

"I can get more if needed," she said. "Come on, let's go back inside."

He found comfort in the sound of her voice. She guided him back to the dining room area. He sat down.

"Lift your shirt, and I'll clean the wound." She held up the other cup.

He complied. But a moment later, he gritted his teeth as the water ran over his cut.

"Can you tell how bad it is?"

"Not in this light," she said softly.

He put his shirt down and leaned back.

She took a seat in the booth that no longer had a table. "I don't know how long until sunrise. It's still pretty dark out there."

It would be pointless for them to stumble around in the black of night. They might end up even more lost. "Maybe we could both rest for a bit," he said.

He rose to his feet and found a booth that would allow him to put his legs up on a wooden crate. He leaned his head against the boarded-up window and closed his eyes. Hope did the same.

From across the room, he could hear her breathing get heavier. Gradually, his mind calmed and the need to sleep overtook the pain of the cut, which didn't hurt much if he remained still.

He slept.

Hours later, he awoke to sunlight streaming through a tiny crack where the wood on the window had been torn away.

And then he heard the sound of a car rolling by on the road. The engine stopped.

His mind cleared instantly. He jumped to his feet and rushed over to Hope, who was still asleep. The rest had done him good. He was not in as much pain.

He shook her shoulder. "Hope, wake up. Someone's outside."

The boarded windows meant there was no way to see out. Maybe it was someone who could help them…or not.

She responded with incoherent mumbling.

"Hope, come on. We'd better hide until we're sure it's not the man who wants you dead."

He prayed it wasn't the assassin. Despite his injury, he'd see that no harm came to her.

Hope felt like she was swimming upward through brain fog. Exhaustion had caused her to fall into a deep sleep.

The warmth of Andrew's hand as he pulled on hers woke her up a little.

"Someone's outside. Hurry, I just heard a door slam."

Only his touch, the way he held her hand, kept the panic at bay.

He led her toward the back door. The sunlight nearly blinded her when they stepped outside. She heard footsteps as they ran deeper into the trees.

They crouched behind a tree. Andrew peered out, then moved forward to look around the building. He returned seconds later, leaning close and whispering in her ear. "It's him. He's found us."

Her heart beat faster as she tensed up.

"We have to get to his car before he comes back out." He grabbed her hand. "It's the only way we can get away from him."

They moved through the trees at a diagonal from the building. How long would it take Jason to search the three areas of the building's interior? Maybe five minutes. A little longer if he moved some of the larger objects around to see if they were hiding behind them. They'd left no evidence behind that they had been there. He might just take a quick look and leave.

They emerged from the trees. The car was parked just outside the building in what used to be the parking lot but now was broken concrete.

Andrew swung the driver's side door open. She got into the back seat on the same side, not wanting to risk wasting time to run around to the passenger side of the front seat.

When she looked over her shoulder, Jason was jogging toward the car. The assassin broke into a run.

"He's coming!" She glanced at the dashboard. There was no key in the ignition.

"I just need a second." Andrew's attention was on the underside of the dashboard. He must be trying to hotwire the car.

Her door flung open and Jason reached in to grab her. She swung her legs and kicked the assassin in his face. He grabbed her feet and tried to drag her out of the car.

She kicked kangaroo style, hitting him in the chest and shoulders.

The car started up.

The assassin pulled his knife from the sheath and lifted it to drive it into Andrew's back.

"Andrew!" Hope screamed in warning.

Andrew turned his head, eyes growing wide and round.

She lunged forward and pushed the assassin's arm that held the knife. It struck the back of the headrest and fell out of Jason's hand.

As the car rolled forward, the man held on to the door. He half climbed in and grabbed Hope's shirt at the stomach, trying to pull her out.

She tried to get away in the confined space while the car gained speed. The assassin was running alongside the car as it went faster. He crawled in. The back car door was still open. Jason climbed on top of Hope and placed his hand on her neck.

His face was red with rage as he choked her. "You need to come with me."

"Get away from her!" Andrew stopped the car but left it running. He ran around to the open door and yanked the assassin off Hope. "She's not going anywhere with you."

The two men wrestled on the ground. Jason ended up on top of Andrew, pummeling his face and chest.

Fear seized Hope. Andrew was going to be knocked out if she didn't act fast. With his injury, he would be less able to fight back.

She jumped out of the back seat and looked around for something to hit the assassin with. The knife lay on the floor of the back seat. She picked it up, but hesitated. She'd never stabbed anyone in her life.

She had to save Andrew.

Her jab to Jason's left shoulder was weak but enough for him to grip his arm and draw his attention to Hope, who took a step back. Andrew was able to roll out from underneath the assailant and get to his knees. While Jason's attention was directed toward Hope, Andrew karate chopped the man on the side of the neck in such a way that it hit a nerve and then he jabbed him in the solar plexus, knocking the wind out of him.

Hope had already retreated toward the open driver's side door. She jumped in and shifted into Drive. In the side-view mirror, she saw Andrew sprinting toward the car and signaling with his hand that she needed to start driving.

She rolled forward as he jumped into the back seat and pulled the door shut. The assassin swayed, lifting himself to his feet and pulling out his phone. He must be calling for help.

Once on the gravel road, she pressed the gas. She didn't see anything up ahead but more forest and old road. She had to trust that they were headed back to civilization and that they would make it before the hit man brought in reinforcements.

SIX

Exhausted and in pain from the cut on his stomach, Andrew slumped in the back seat trying to catch his breath. Despite that, he was amazed at how hard Hope had fought for their survival and escape. It seemed the schoolteacher had inner strength that even she hadn't realized she had.

He lifted his chin to see through the windshield. In the early morning light, the lake came into view, but he saw no sign of people anywhere. This was the less commercial side of the lake.

"I guess I'll just keep driving." Hope kept her eyes on the road up ahead. "Back into town, right? This road must go around the lake."

Jason Zimmerman was probably counting on them returning to Whitetail. Did he have another contact in town who would come after them or had he been calling for a ride? Zimmerman knew which direction they were driving and could guess at where they would enter Whitetail. Andrew considered the options.

He sat up a little straighter, gripping the back of the front seat. "Maybe that is not such a good idea."

As they drew closer to the lake, several boats came into view.

She slowed down. "What do you suggest?"

His cut caused a stab of pain every time he moved. Andrew lifted his shirt where dried blood had crusted. He needed to disinfect it as soon as possible.

The attacker could identify the car they'd taken from him. Andrew needed a moment to plan. "Pull over." He glanced over his shoulder, not seeing any car approaching from behind.

Hope took a dirt spur road that brought them closer to the lake. She killed the engine and shifted in her seat to face him. Her expression changed when she looked at him. "Are you okay?"

"I need to clean this cut and get a dressing on it. Stuff we can get at a pharmacy."

"Are you sure you don't want to see a doctor?" Her voice filled with worry. "You look really pale."

He lifted his shirt so she could see the cut. "I don't think it's deep enough to require stitches. I just need to clean it and cover it, so it doesn't get infected."

Her forehead still wrinkled with concern. "If you say so."

"While we're stopped, let's search the car. It belongs to the man who tried to kill you. Let's see if we can find any evidence as to who hired him."

"*Hired* him? I assumed it was the Queen Bee Cartel." She reached over and opened the glove compartment. "Nothing in there, not even registration." She turned so she could look right at him. "Jason is coming after me because the cartel wants revenge, right?"

"It's a little more complicated than that." He couldn't keep her in the dark any longer. "Zimmerman was also in witness protection. But he was placed in a small town in Washington."

Hope stared at him for a long moment as if she was trying to comprehend what he was saying. "Let me see if I got this right." Light came into her eyes and she spoke slowly, "Whoever is behind this used a guy in the Witness Protection Program to come after me. He knew exactly where to find me. That means someone who works for the program and has access to all the information about me and is probably connected to the cartel."

Andrew nodded. "Unfortunately, someone was able to acquire some highly classified information about your new identity."

"It's like being in limbo. I can't just go a get a new identity, and I can't go back to my old life." She took in an intense breath. "Both would only end up putting me in more danger."

He placed his hand over hers where it rested on the back of the seat, hoping it would alleviate some of the fear he heard in her voice. "Look, I trust my direct supervisor, Bryson Whitman. Maybe he will be able to ferret out what is going on. But no matter what, I'm here with you, Hope. I vowed I'd keep you safe until we can get this resolved, and I intend to keep that promise."

Her round eyes locked to his and he squeezed her hand. "I know you will." She sighed and shook her head. "That Jason guy kept asking what I had done with my brother's things."

"You mean the stuff in Craig's house?"

"I guess. The thing is, I don't know exactly what happened to it. I was taken to a safe house almost immediately once the police learned I could identify the man who shot Craig. I assume that one of my brother's friends or our godfather took care of it. We don't have any close relatives who live in New Mexico."

Andrew sat up straighter. "Wasn't Craig killed because of drug-related debt?"

"That is what the police thought. But every time I saw Craig, he was sober and had been for months."

"Maybe the reason he was killed is more complicated than the police realized." Andrew peered out the back window, half expecting to see a car racing toward them. He was starting to formulate a plan for what they needed to do. "Let's go into town, get some things for my cut and ditch this car. It will be too easy to find us in it. And then we need to leave town as quickly as possible." He pushed open the back door and got in the front passenger seat. "Do you have the keys for the car you were issued?"

She thought for a moment. "I dropped them in the struggle."

Going back to the apartment was probably a bad idea anyway.

Starting the engine, Hope pulled back out onto the road that wound around the lake. Gradually, they saw more cars, boats and people. The town of Whitetail was just waking up as they came to the edge of it.

"I'm not sure how we will get out of town. I didn't see any car rental places in Whitetail. The nearest airport is fifty miles from here."

"From what I saw, you can rent almost any kind of watercraft you can imagine," she said. Hope drove through town until she spotted a drugstore and parked.

He pushed open the car door.

She got out of the car as well and walked beside him into the drugstore. Andrew grabbed some gauze, disinfectant, over-the-counter pain medication and a phone.

They made their way up to the counter to pay

for the items. When he stared out the window, a blond man he didn't recognize had pulled into the parking lot and was looking at Jason's car.

Andrew turned away from the window and whispered in Hope's ear, "I think we better leave out the back exit."

The clerk handed Andrew his bagged merchandise. Adrenaline coursed through his body as they hurried down an aisle toward the back door.

The door opened up to an alley where there was a dumpster. When they walked to the end of the alley, he could see the marina off in the distance. Renting a boat seemed like the best option for getting away fast.

He estimated it to be a twenty-minute walk to the marina. They slipped out from the protection of the alley and stepped onto the street. They walked several blocks. When they were about to turn up a street, he dared himself a glance back at the drugstore parking lot. The blond man who had taken an interest in Jason's car was still in the parking lot. A sure sign that he'd been sent to watch for them to come out.

It was probably just a matter of seconds before he would conclude they had fled through a different door.

Hope glanced in the direction of his gaze. Her face drained of color when she saw the man in the parking lot.

"We better hurry," Andrew said.

Touching Hope's elbow, he guided her around the corner out of view of the man who had been sent to get them.

Hope's heart pounded as they turned the corner. Now Jason had an accomplice. Maybe the man had been sent merely to track them until the hit man could set up another attack or the other man had the same skill set as Jason and would follow them and wait for an opportunity to kill them once they weren't around people.

They walked at a brisk pace as the marina drew closer. Running might call attention to them. But being out in the open caused her nerves to be raw. Every noise made her jump. From a woman yelling at her friend half a block away to a car revving up on the street.

They got to the edge of the marina. Andrew stopped as he scanned the huge parking lot and the water beyond.

She searched the area as well, spotting a hut that had the same logo as the boats that were available for rental. "There."

They hurried across the parking lot. When they got to the hut, the window was closed. The posted hours sign indicated they would not be open for another half hour, plenty of time for someone to search the parking lot and spot them.

She took in a breath to stave off the rising panic. "What do we do now?"

He pointed toward a coffee hut that was open. "Let's get something to drink and find a way to hide in plain sight. Plus, I need to take care of this cut."

They walked over to the coffee hut and put in their order. After the barista closed the window to make the coffee, Andrew pointed toward a bench that faced the water. "Sit there with your back to the parking lot. I won't be far from you, but right now they are looking for a man and woman together. If someone does come looking for us, it is less likely to register who we are if we're not in close proximity."

The barista opened the window and handed them the coffees. Andrew asked to buy one of the baseball hats that had the coffee hut logo on it. "Not much of a disguise," he admitted as he put it on. Their clothes, the brightly colored T-shirt and board shorts they'd gotten at the Lakeside Inn, were like a flashing neon sign.

He studied her for a long moment. "Take your hair out of the ponytail," he said.

She removed the scrunchie from her hair. "Better?"

A faint smile graced his face when he looked at her in a way that wasn't just scrutinizing her makeshift disguise. She raised an eyebrow, enjoying the unexpected spark of attraction between them. "Well?"

Color rose up in his cheeks. "Oh…yeah…best we can do on short notice." He pointed toward the bench. "I won't let you out of my sight even when I clean and dress this cut. It's only a half hour. Keep your eyes on the water, don't give away that you are nervous or looking for anyone."

Gripping her coffee, she headed toward the bench and sat down. She took several sips of her iced latte, enjoying the creamy sweetness, while she watched the seagulls dive at the water and boats heading out for the day. In her peripheral vision, she could see Andrew as he sat on a bench and took care of his cut.

She watched a mom with a stroller play with her toddler on the beach, helping the little boy fill a bucket with sand and tip it over for the start of a sandcastle. A sweet scene between mother and child that she wondered if she would ever experience. Probably not.

It had surprised her that when Andrew looked at her a moment ago, she had seen appreciation in his eyes. While the warmth that had passed between them brought a smile to her face, she knew that in the grand scheme of events, nothing could ever come of it.

Once the corruption within WITSEC was found, she would be given a new identity and a new place to live. Andrew might not even be her contact person again. That could put her back in danger.

She listened to a boat engine grow fainter. As the vessel headed toward deep water, sadness washed over her. Even once she was settled into a new life somewhere, any relationship would be fraught with the need to hide who she really was. Which meant a long-term romance was off-limits. And even the friendships she forged could not be truly close, because she could never be free to really be herself. But to reveal her past meant risking her own safety as well as the other person's. She saw a lonely life ahead.

However, she was grateful that no matter whom she had to pretend to be, God knew the real Hope fully and intimately. That truth was her only comfort.

A hand cupped her shoulder. "I got the boat. We can go now." The warmth of Andrew's touch seeped through her skin.

She tilted her head to look up at the handsome US marshal, who had pulled the baseball cap low over his face. There was that smile again.

She rose from the bench. Andrew walked between her and the parking lot. A car moved slowly through the lot as though looking for someone.

"All they had to rent was either a motorboat

or something huge that one man couldn't handle. I'd hoped for something that would allow you to hide but we will take what we can get." He led her to a place on the dock where there were several motorboats with the rental logo.

After hopping into the boat, he held his hand out for her.

She climbed aboard, then picked up one of the two life jackets that were in the boat while he yanked the cord to start the motor. Once the engine chug-chugged and then sputtered to life, he sped away from the pier out into the water.

Though he had not shared it with her, Andrew appeared to have a plan. She had noticed him studying the maps of the lake that were posted several times while they had waited for the rental place to open up.

He did his job so well, but after the moment of attraction between them, she found herself wanting to know more about him besides who he was as a marshal. He wasn't a man that gave much away about who he was on a personal level.

From where she sat on the front seat, she glanced back at the parking lot, still not able to believe that they had not been followed. Jason Zimmerman had been relentless so far and now he had help. She knew one thing for sure. The assassins weren't going to give up easily.

SEVEN

As he traveled farther from shore, Andrew tried to move toward where there was boat traffic while keeping his destination in mind. In order to stay safe, he needed to not get isolated on the water. Other people provided a degree of protection.

Though he had not told Hope, he had seen the man from the drugstore skulking through the parking lot as they got into the motorboat. His distinct blond hair made him easy to spot. No need to make Hope more fearful. It was just a matter of time before someone came after her.

He felt a growing affection for her that went beyond his job that made him even more protective toward her.

The motorboat scuttled over the rough water, bouncing and catching air. Once he was sure they were in the clear and had not been followed, he would try to contact Bryson on his private cell. After he activated the phone, he'd tried once while they waited on the shore but had gotten no answer.

By studying the maps, he'd gotten a feel for the area around the lake. There was a place on the north side accessible only by boat where people gathered to eat and enjoy the beach. It was a weekday, but hopefully there would be enough of a breakfast crowd to provide a degree of protection from the assassin and his cohort coming after them. They could get something to eat and maybe different, more low-key clothes, and make the phone call. Then take the boat to where they might be able to catch a ride with someone out of town.

Other boats marked with the rental logo swirled around them as he headed toward the north shore. He didn't have much of a chance to see who was at the helm of each one.

Up ahead, he saw his destination. The beach had only a few people lying on towels or playing in the surf in the early morning coolness.

Beyond the beach was a series of hut-like buildings with people sitting at outdoor tables and milling around.

He slowed as he drew closer to shore, docking between two larger vessels. Hope glanced over her shoulder after he killed the engine. The boat swayed and bobbed in the water.

"What is the plan?" she asked.

"Let's grab some breakfast. I need to call Bryson and find out what he's come up with."

They made their way to shore and then took the trail that led up to the eateries. After grabbing a breakfast muffin, Andrew searched for a place where he'd be able to have a private conversation with his boss while still utilizing the security of the crowd.

They found an outdoor table that was separated from the others but still had a view of the growing morning group of people.

Hope took a chair opposite him. The sun caught the blond highlights in her hair. As she took a bite of her muffin, he was struck by how pretty she was.

As much as he could, he'd been watching other boats when they came in. One in particular held his interest. The boat had come in minutes after they had docked. It was large enough to have a below-deck area. So far, no one had disembarked.

This time when Andrew called, his supervisor picked up.

"Hey, saw you called earlier. I was out jogging. Figured you'd get hold of me when you could," Bryson said.

"Did you find out anything?"

"I had our IT people look for the possibility of a hack from the outside." He paused for a moment. Andrew could hear him let out a breath. "It doesn't look like that is what happened."

He closed his eyes and gripped the phone

tighter. So much for hoping that someone in the program wasn't corrupt. "I don't even know who would have access to Hope's file."

"The WITSEC case manager would be the one who put together the whole file that you see, but there would also be people who worked on creating a new ID and finding a viable relocation spot."

"So a bunch of people would have pieces of the puzzle," Andrew mused.

Again, Bryson didn't speak right away. He pictured his friend/boss pacing in his office. "The thing is, it could be anyone in the organization if they got access to the case manager's passwords or had a way to hack in."

Hope, who had been staring out at the lake while she munched her muffin, swiveled in her chair and gripped his arm. She pointed down at the shore.

Andrew didn't see anything. He pulled the phone away from his face.

She leaned close to him. "I saw a man who looked like Jason Zimmerman."

"Gotta go," Andrew said, abruptly ending the call. He left his half-eaten muffin behind. Grabbing Hope's hand, he headed toward where there were more people.

He hadn't seen Zimmerman, but he would trust Hope's instincts. They couldn't risk being spotted. He led her into a small gift shop.

Hope pressed close to him. "What do we do now?"

He peered at all the colorful T-shirts advertising the various tourist spots around Whitetail. He grabbed the only two gray T-shirts he saw. "First of all, we stop dressing like a flashing neon sign." As an afterthought, he grabbed a hat for her.

Andrew paid for the shirts and hat, and they changed quickly. When they turned to face the glass storefront, he had a view of Jason Zimmerman as he walked by, his attention on the boardwalk filled with people.

He took a step back into the store, addressing the store clerk. "Is there a back door?"

The clerk shook his head.

They both shrank away from the window and watched outside for a long moment. They couldn't wait here forever. It was just a matter of time before the killer searched the interior of the shops. He touched Hope's elbow and whispered, "Let's try to go back to that boat and get out of here. I need to finish my conversation with Bryson."

Both of them pulled their hats low over their faces as they stepped out into the morning sun.

They hurried toward the single-file trail that led down to the docks. In order to get into the boat quickly, Hope stepped into the shallow water and swung her leg over the side. Andrew jumped in as well and pulled the cord.

The engine roared to life, and he eased out of the space between the two larger boats. Hope held on to her hat as they gained speed.

He guided the boat toward a cluster of other vessels, hoping to disappear into the crowd. When he looked over his shoulder, he saw a larger boat backing out of a spot.

Hope shouted above the sputter of the motor. "I'm pretty sure that's him."

The look of intense fear evident in her features sliced right through him. He had to get her out of here fast.

Andrew aimed toward a larger vessel and then curved around it. Any hiding place would be temporary. The motorboat bounced through the choppy water created by multiple wakes. He moved to avoid the early morning water skiers out to get some runs in before it was too hot.

They headed toward a distant shore that looked like it connected with part of Whitetail. His hope had been to get away from here as quickly as possible. He needed to talk to his boss to try to set up some sort of highly classified safe house for Hope.

When he peered over his shoulder, the larger boat moved steadily toward them.

Hope did not have to see the man at the helm of the boat clearly to know that it was Jason Zimmerman who was headed their way, systematically hunting her down. From a distance, she could discern his muscular build.

The hit man made no pretense of hiding. Being in plain sight was probably part of his intimidation strategy.

Andrew came into the shore and docked the boat. The rentals were set up so that they could be tracked and picked up later by the rental company.

Once he was on land, he reached out a hand to help her. A long line of boats like beads on a necklace wound around the shore where they had docked. She could see Zimmerman's boat chugging toward them and disappearing several boat lengths from where they had stopped.

Andrew held her hand, and she drew closer to him with a nervous sideways glance. "What are we going to do?"

"We have to get you out of this town, find a secure place for you to hide. But first we need to go talk to the sheriff, see if I can get you some additional protection in order to do that." The steadiness of his grip calmed her. "I thought maybe we would just try to catch a ride, but I think that would be too dangerous now."

He hurried them along the beach until it intersected with stone stairs that led back into Whitetail proper. Once they were in an area where there were businesses, he pulled her into a boutique where the woman had just flipped the sign to Open. They slipped back away from the window.

The lady who had opened up the shop stepped toward Hope. "Can I help you?"

Hope absently lifted the sleeve of a silky dress. "Just looking, thank you."

The woman made her way back to the counter. "If you have any questions, just let me know."

Andrew checked his phone. Hope stepped closer to him so they would not be overheard. He was looking at a map of Whitetail.

"The sheriff's office isn't too far from here," Andrew whispered. "He would have been informed about you arriving here."

When she glanced out the window, Jason Zimmerman stalked past them, his gaze focused on something unseen in the distance. Her heart pounded as the breath caught in her throat. She reached for the security of Andrew's hand.

Feeling the weight of the boutique owner's stare, Hope turned her attention to pretending to be interested in a linen shirt. "This is pretty, don't you think?" she said to Andrew, who only glanced in her direction.

"Yeah, it's nice."

Though he did not continue to look directly out the window, she could tell that was where most of his focus was. Would Jason realize he'd missed them and backtrack?

"Are you folks from out of town?" The boutique owner busied herself with setting up a display of scarves.

Simultaneously Hope said, "Yes," and Andrew replied, "No."

The boutique owner placed a scarf on the counter and looked at both of them. "Well, which is it?"

Hope piped up. "I'm from here. He's from out of town."

Now for sure they had made themselves memorable to this lady. If Jason came back here and questioned her, she would have no trouble remembering that she had seen them.

"We should get going." Andrew ushered her toward the door.

Once back out on the sunny street, she glanced in the direction the assailant had been traveling.

"Let's go this way." Andrew indicated a side street where they were less likely to be spotted. As they stepped past the side window of the boutique, Hope caught a glimpse of the owner still watching them.

Andrew led her on a circuitous route down alleys and side streets. He stopped to check his phone several times. The sheriff's office was at the end of Main Street sandwiched between an insurance office and a photographer's studio that featured oversize landscape pictures of the mountains and lakes of Montana.

After glancing up and down the street, Andrew pushed the door open and stepped inside the sheriff's office. Only a single light over a desk had been left on. An overhead fan whirred above them.

"Hello?" Andrew stepped deeper into the interior of the main office.

The front windows were huge with a clear view into the interior, which made Hope nervous. Jason could walk right by and see them inside. "I don't think anyone is here."

Andrew signaled for her to come farther into the room. "There's a hallway here. It's quiet… I need to finish my call to Bryson. Looks like the sheriff just stepped out for a minute. Maybe he'll be back by the time I'm done."

Hope pressed her back against the wall and stared at the ceiling.

Andrew touched buttons on his phone. "Hey, sorry I had to be so abrupt. This hired gun is on us like cold on a Popsicle. Is there someplace safe close by I could take Hope until we can get this resolved?"

Andrew listened for a moment before responding.

"Yes, but we don't know the source of the leak

or what kind of access they have. Is there any way to get her to a safe house without it being in our computer system?"

Andrew listened and nodded. "How long would that take?" He fell silent. "Okay, I'll give you a call after you have time to set things up. Stay in touch, Bryson. I will hold on to this phone for now."

He pressed the disconnect button.

She gazed at him. "What did your boss say?"

"That it would be impossible to go to an established witness protection safe house and not have someone in the organization know about it. There is always paperwork involved." He blew out a frustrated breath. "But he is going to talk to other agencies who work in this region to try to get us some help."

"I keep wondering why Jason was asking about my brother's things. Isn't that something we need to figure out?"

"That might be an investigation down the line. Right now, my priority has to be getting you to a secure location." Andrew paced up the hall and peered around the corner. The look on his face indicated that no one had come into the sheriff's office.

"What did your boss suggest in the meantime?"

"We need to get out of Whitetail. Then find a place to hide until Bryson can set something up."

"We don't have a car," she reminded him. "The car rental place is at the airport fifty miles away."

"That's okay, because we've already learned that a car isn't the safest place to be. It would be better if we stayed with a crowd. I saw buses with the names of tours all over this town the night I dropped you off." He had already pulled his phone out and was typing in something.

She stood close to him so she could peer over his shoulder, feeling his body heat. A trickle of awareness went through her but she forced herself to focus on the matter at hand. Three bus tour companies based out of Whitetail came up on the screen. He pointed to his screen. "This one has tours of Glacier Park that leave twice a day. It looks like the next one is in less than an hour." He clicked onto a map.

"The pickup site looks like it's not too far from here."

"Yes, I see that," Andrew said. "Our other option is to wait around here and hope the sheriff shows up. He could provide us with a ride to somewhere."

She stared out through the big windows. "What if he doesn't come back until the end of the day, and we've missed our chance to get out of town? What if the tour fills up?"

He nodded slowly. "The longer we stay around here, the more dangerous it becomes. This is not a big city. What is there, five thousand people in this town?"

"Just a shade under six, according to the guidebook," she replied. "But they get thousands of tourists and people with vacation homes, especially in the summer."

He smiled. "So glad someone did that research."

She lifted her chin slightly. "I can't help myself. I'm a teacher. I'm curious."

"I'm just glad you are." His voice filled with affection.

Andrew checked the map on his phone one more time before they stepped back out on the street.

Staying alert, they walked at a brisk pace. The sidewalks had begun to fill with people.

Hope wasn't sure what made her glance across the street. Maybe it was some instinct for survival. Her eyes went to a candy shop where a crowd had just dispersed. Jason Zimmerman locked eyes with her for only a second before slipping behind a mother with two kids. The momentary glare gave her chills.

"I see him." Andrew grabbed her arm at the elbow. "Let's get out of here as fast as we can." His voice held a note of urgency.

EIGHT

Andrew led Hope down a side street, knowing that it would be a detour on their way to where the bus tour picked up people. They still had time to get there. Hopefully all the seats would not be filled. First, he had to make sure that Zimmerman did not follow them.

When he peered over his shoulder, he could see the man's head bob above a cluster of teenage girls. He was going to be harder to shake than Andrew had thought. If they slipped into a shop, Zimmerman would see them.

Hope let out a tiny cry and pointed up ahead. Zimmerman's blond henchman was in front of them. Certainly, they wouldn't try anything with people around, not something other people could witness.

"Zimmerman has a knife, remember?" Hope's voice laced with fear.

How could he forget? The memory made the

cut across his stomach throb. "We can't let him get close to us."

He led Hope across the street knowing they'd be followed. He was trying to buy time, to come up with a plan. They stepped inside a bookshop where an older woman was browsing the shelves. A tall, thin man stood at the counter.

Zimmerman waited for them outside the bookshop storefront, his back to them while he watched the street. Andrew hesitated in his step. Going out the back door would probably not be a good idea. Zimmerman had probably already directed his thug to go after them when they stepped into the alley.

He checked his watch. Fifteen minutes until the bus tour left. "We have no choice, Hope. Stay close to me and try to keep where there are people around us."

She nodded as he put a hand on her upper arm above the elbow. The assailant glanced inside the bookshop. Both of them stepped back into the shadows the high shelves created. Andrew waited until Zimmerman turned to look out on the street. A group of three women were about to walk past the shop.

Andrew opened the door and stepped in front of them with Hope at his side. The move meant he nearly crashed into the women. He wrapped his arm around Hope's back and drew her close, desiring to keep her safe from the dangerous man behind them.

They walked briskly and turned the corner where there were fewer people. The three women had turned as well, shielding them from Zimmerman's view. Andrew had no idea where the blond thug was. He could see the bus tour kiosk up ahead and the bus for the Glacier tour parked by it. They hurried across the street.

People were already boarding as they approached the kiosk. The young woman wearing a visor that advertised the tour company smiled when they stepped up to the window. "Are there any tickets left for the tour?"

"I have exactly four open seats."

"Any together?"

She studied her computer. "I can put you behind each other. Both are aisle seats."

"That will do," Andrew said. He paid the lady.

She gave him the printed tickets with the seat numbers. "Sometimes people are open to trading seats if they are by themselves."

"Thank you." He smiled.

"Enjoy the tour."

The bus was nearly full by the time they boarded and found their seats. Hope took the seat closer to the driver, and he settled into the one behind her.

The driver got into his seat and turned the key

in the ignition, allowing the bus to idle while he wrote in a logbook. Then he set the book to one side and reached for the handle to close the door on the bus.

"Wait!" someone shouted from outside.

The driver held on to the handle but stopped closing the door. The final passenger got on. Jason Zimmerman smiled at them, metal teeth glistening as he stood at the front of the bus. He glanced at his ticket and walked up the aisle.

Hope sat up straighter. Andrew's heart pounded as the man walked past them, making sure to brush both their shoulders on the way. Zimmerman took a seat in the row opposite of where they were, four seats behind them.

The bus rolled forward and turned out onto the road. Within a few minutes, they were at the edge of Whitetail and taking the exit that led to the highway.

If he turned his head slightly, Andrew could see Jason's shoulder and outside leg.

The bus driver picked up his radio and welcomed everyone to the tour. "We have about an hour drive to the park. We will stop briefly just outside the park for a chance to stretch your legs, pick up a snack or use the amenities."

The driver continued to talk about what they would see in the park until his voice became background noise to Andrew. He doubted the hit man would try anything while they were on the bus, but he would be looking for his chance to get to Hope. Something Andrew would prevent at all costs.

He took his phone out and texted Bryson.

Any news on a safe house for Hope?

His phone dinged before he even had a chance to put it back in his pocket.

Working on it. I've got an FBI friend who owes me a favor and lives in that part of the country. Where are you now?

Just left Whitetail. Headed toward Glacier on a bus.

Get off as soon as you can. My friend can come to you. I sent him to Whitetail.

Assassin is on the bus with us.

Be careful. Call me as soon as you stop.

Andrew leaned forward in the seat and touched the shoulder of the man who was sitting with Hope. "Excuse me... I should have asked before we started rolling. I wonder if you wouldn't mind switching seats, so I can sit next to my girlfriend?"

"Oh sure, no problem," the guy said.

Andrew stood up, which allowed him to a get full view of Zimmerman. The cold look in his eyes made Andrew's stomach lurch. He was in the way of the shooter getting to Hope. He had no doubt that Zimmerman would kill him the first chance he got.

Andrew stepped to one side so the man could get to his seat. Hope scooted toward the window.

Once Andrew sat down, she leaned close to him and whispered, "Hey, boyfriend." There was a note of levity in her voice. "That's our cover, right?"

He liked the idea of being her boyfriend even if it was for show. It was the first time he'd felt that way since his wife had died though he knew it couldn't ever be real. He whispered back, "I suppose it's less shocking than announcing that I am your protection against the assassin four seats behind you."

"I saw you texting. I wondered if there was anything I needed to know."

Andrew took out the phone and allowed her to scroll through the texts. She nodded in understanding and then handed it back to him.

They rolled down the highway. The miles clicked by. Andrew kept his attention tuned to

Jason's movements, which he could track in his peripheral vision.

The bus slowed, and he heard the turn signal going just before it veered off the road into a large parking lot. Their stop consisted of a convenience store gas station that also sold items needed for fishing. Plus, there were several stands that sold farm produce, including flathead cherries, as well as handcrafted items. On the other side of the roadside stop were a motor home park and a few stick-built houses. He could see a lake off in the distance.

The bus driver stopped and opened the door. "Okay, folks, you have twenty minutes. Next stop... Glacier Park."

Andrew stood up and moved out into the aisle. He gestured for Hope to get in front of him.

He heard an "Excuse me" behind him. When he turned his head, he saw that there was only one person between him and the killer. Several other cars were parked by the convenience store. Once the bus passengers had all disembarked, the area was filled with people.

From the moment they stepped off the bus, it was clear that Zimmerman intended to stay close to them and look for an opportunity to strike.

Andrew could feel the weight of the man's lethal gaze. He wrapped an arm around Hope and led her inside the little store. With Zimmerman hanging so close, talking on the phone would not be an option. Andrew and Hope stood near the counter where the clerk was and where he could see outside.

He texted his boss as to the location they were waiting at. People milled through the little store grabbing drinks and snacks and looking at the souvenirs.

His boss did not text back right away. He only hoped that the information would get relayed to the FBI agent as quickly as possible.

The other passengers slowly exited the store and boarded the bus. The driver paid for a bottled water and looked at them.

"You folks coming?"

"I think our plans have changed."

The driver shrugged and then glanced down the aisle where Zimmerman had a clear view of them while he pretended to be looking at the candy.

The bus stirred up dust as it pulled back out to the road. The last car exited the lot, leaving only the clerk and the hit man inside.

Zimmerman stepped outside, sitting on a bench by the door. They would not be able to leave the store without walking past him.

Andrew checked his phone again, hoping to see a text from Bryson.

The clerk watched them for a long moment,

probably wondering why they weren't leaving or at least buying something. A car pulled into the lot. The driver did not get out.

Hope must have sensed that they were making the clerk nervous. She walked down an aisle and grabbed two flavored waters. She handed them to Andrew, who stepped up to the counter to pay for them.

"We're waiting for a ride," he explained as the clerk handed him his change.

"It's none of my business." The clerk tilted his head toward where Zimmerman sat outside. "Something feels really off about those two guys out there, the one on the bench and the one just sitting in his car. We were robbed a few weeks ago. I have a gun under the counter."

Andrew stepped a little closer to the window, trying to get a better look at the man behind the wheel. He saw now that the man was the same thug who had been helping Zimmerman before.

The men were just waiting for the opportunity to come after him and Hope.

As the minutes ticked away, Hope could feel herself growing more tense. Andrew checked his phone several times. The look on his face made it clear that he had not heard from his boss yet.

Was help even on the way?

Jason lifted his chin as some sort of signal to

the man in the car. It was the blond man who had stared them down on the street in Whitetail.

Andrew took a step back from the window. His arm went in front of her protectively. The clerk had gone into a back room only moments before. The man must have seen his opportunity.

Just then, a car pulled into the lot. A man and a woman exited their car. Jason sat back down on the bench.

By the time the man and woman had entered the store, the clerk returned and stood behind the counter.

Andrew checked his phone and then showed the text to Hope.

Agent Valdez is about twenty minutes away.

Hope let out a relieved breath, watching as several cars came and went. Another bus showed up and the place was once again teeming with people. Jason stood up and glared at them through the window before retreating to the car where the thug sat behind the wheel.

There were still several cars in the lot when a dark SUV pulled up and a man in jeans and a cowboy hat got out and looked around. Despite the pants and the large belt buckle, something about the crispness of his pale blue button-down shirt screamed FBI agent.

"That's got to be Agent Valdez," Andrew whispered.

They stepped outside. Agent Valdez's gaze fixated on the car with the two men in it before he turned his attention to Hope and Andrew.

Though the second bus had already left, there was a car in the lot and another that had parked by one of the souvenir stands.

Andrew approached the other man. "Agent Valdez?"

"Yes." The agent signaled with his eyes that he was aware of the threat in the car. "Looks like we're going to have to take the scenic route to shake those guys."

He led them to the car, where Andrew opened the back door for Hope. "Safer for you back here," he said. "Sit in the middle."

"Thank you." Her voice broke. The realization that where Andrew had directed her to sit was the safest place from a bullet coming into the car made her stomach tighten.

She was glad that he was here with her, at least. Not just because he was a marshal but because she was growing quite fond of him.

Hope settled in and drew her seat belt across her lap while Andrew got into the front passenger seat. The tinted windows meant no one could see in.

Agent Valdez pulled out onto the road. Within

minutes, she saw the black sedan belonging to Jason and the thug looming behind them with only one car between them.

Agent Valdez checked his rearview mirror frequently. It was clear he was aware they were being followed.

"I don't know the whole story with you two. Bryson Whitman just said he needed for you guys to go to a safe house that wouldn't be on WITSEC's radar."

When the exit for the first small town came up, Valdez took it, driving down the main street for only a few blocks before weaving through the side streets. Probably part of his strategy to lose the men who were tailing them.

He got back on the highway and continued to drive. Hope turned her head and checked through the back window several times. There was enough traffic that the assassin could hang back a few cars and not be seen.

Also, he could have been waiting for them at the on-ramp.

She took a deep breath, wishing the tension in her chest would subside. Jason had been tenacious up to this point in coming after her. She dare not let her guard down. And she wasn't about to give up. Somehow this man and the people who sent him had to be stopped. Craig's life could not be in vain. And she wasn't going to die at the assassin's hand.

Valdez and Andrew talked about the fishing and camping they had done in this part of the country. A sort of passion and warmth filled Andrew's voice when he talked about being in the outdoors. It was the first hint she had gotten of who he was as person outside of his work.

She liked the sound of his voice.

Twice more Agent Valdez wove through a town. The second time he did not get back on the interstate. They were on a two-lane road with only a few other cars. None that looked like Jason's vehicle. Maybe they'd finally shaken him.

It was late afternoon by the time the FBI agent pulled up to a series of cabins set far apart and surrounding a lake. He must have decided they had not been followed.

"This is it," Valdez announced. "I can arrange for a car to be dropped off for you in the next few hours, but I have to get back to Bozeman to interview a suspect."

Andrew turned his head, taking in the surroundings. "Sounds good."

There was a note of hesitation in his voice. Maybe he didn't like the idea of being here without a car.

Andrew shook Valdez's hand. "Thanks for your help."

"I'll get that car to you as fast as I can." He opened his console and handed Andrew a key that had a tiny stick for the key chain. "The place should be stocked with the basics."

Andrew got out and opened the door for Hope. She listened to Valdez's tires crunch on the gravel as he drove away. In total there were eight cabins. She saw a vehicle parked outside of two others and one of those was across the lake.

They were in the middle of nowhere without transportation.

Andrew led her to the cabin and put the key in the lock. The door swung open, and they stepped inside. The place was decorated in a rustic country style with checked fabric curtains and seat cushions. It was one open space with a bed down below and what looked like a bed in the loft. A woodstove was at the center of the room.

"I don't know about you, but I am pretty hungry." He walked over to the kitchen area and opened cupboards.

Following suit, she opened the refrigerator, which contained only condiments. Andrew had placed several cans on the counter, along with some shelf-stable milk and a box of mac and cheese.

"What are you hungry for?"

She pointed toward the can of chili. "That would be the fastest. Just open it up and heat it in a pan."

"Yes, but I think we can do better than that. Have you ever had chili mac?"

"No, but my second graders often spoke fondly of it."

Andrew swung a towel over his shoulders. "Well then, you are in for a treat because chili mac is my specialty. Something I learned to make back in my college days." He opened a couple more cupboards. "In the meantime, I'm going to have to stop my stomach from growling." He pulled out some pudding containers.

"Pudding is dessert. Are you going to have it before the main course?"

"Break the rules. Live dangerously." He stepped toward her, holding one of the puddings. "You want one?"

She liked this side of Andrew, much more relaxed and fun. She noticed, though, that he frequently glanced out the windows. Maybe he was being lighthearted for her benefit. He handed her a plastic spoon.

"This is the kind of snack my second graders like, too," she said.

"Then we will eat in their honor." He sat beside her at the kitchen table with the checked tablecloth. "You miss them, the kids?"

"For sure." Sadness swept over her. "I'll never be in a classroom again."

"Maybe when you are settled into a new life, you can teach Sunday school or something."

She took a spoonful of pudding, enjoying the creamy sweetness. "Maybe, if that ever happens."

Andrew took several bites of pudding. "I can see why this is a favorite of second graders everywhere. This is good stuff." Andrew elbowed her.

The gesture was meant to cheer her up. "Thanks, Andrew." She laughed in spite of the reminder of how chaotic her life had become.

He finished his pudding. "Now, my dear, why don't you sit back and relax and let Chef Andrew take over."

"Are you sure you don't want some help?"

"Why don't you sit in that chair and read," he suggested. "I'll have some food together in no time."

She noticed that he pointed toward the chair that was away from the window back by the bed. Andrew was being pleasant and entertaining, but he hadn't forgotten that her life was under threat. She studied the bookshelf until she found a book of nature essays that looked interesting. Then, sitting back in the shadows underneath the loft, she clicked on a side lamp.

Andrew hummed to himself while he put some water on to boil. His singing stopped abruptly.

She looked up from her book. Andrew hurried toward the window and stood off to one side.

He signaled for Hope to get on the floor. She dropped down by the bed, pressing her back against it. Still gripping the now-closed book, she drew it to her chest.

Andrew lifted the edge of the curtain to peer outside.

She braced herself for the sonic boom of a gunshot, or a broken window or a door being kicked in.

NINE

Andrew knew he had not imagined movement outside the cabin. Someone or something had swept by the window. Yet when he peered outside, the place looked quiet. Other than the windows, the front door was the only way in or out of the cabin.

He debated what to do for only a few seconds.

Identify and neutralize the threat. He turned back toward Hope, who looked small where she rested on the floor. "Lock the door behind me. Then stay at the back of the cabin."

She nodded, though that glazed look had come back into her eyes. "Be careful."

How quickly things changed. Only moments before they had been joking and enjoying each other's company. Now their lives could be in grave jeopardy. He swung open the door and stepped outside, wishing he had thought to ask Agent Valdez to loan him a gun.

The deadbolt clicked behind him. Heart pounding, he circled the cabin. Once he was on the side of the cabin that faced the lake, he thought he had identified what had gone past the windows. A man in a fishing vest stood at the water's edge, casting a line.

He looked up and waved. Andrew waved back. He returned to the cabin and knocked three times. "Hope, it's me."

He heard footsteps and then the door swung open. Her expression radiated tension.

"I think we're all clear for now. It was just a guy headed to go fishing." He stared back at the empty gravel driveway. How long before that car got here?

Andrew stepped back inside.

"I took your pan off the stove. The noodles looked pretty cooked." Hope turned toward the kitchen area.

He had gotten Agent Valdez's number. He texted him and asked if it would be possible to get a gun as well. Phoning would mean he would interrupt Valdez's interview, or the other man might have turned his phone off.

Andrew returned to the stove and completed the meal he had planned. The scare had robbed him of his good mood, though he had relished the sound of Hope's laughter. He watched as she set the table with paper napkins and plates while he finished cooking. She filled two glasses with water. He placed the steaming bowls on the table along with some crackers he'd found.

"Smells amazing," Hope murmured.

"Mind if I say grace?"

Light came into her eyes. "I'd like that."

He had a feeling she was a woman of faith, just something about her. Andrew bowed his head.

"Lord, thank You for this meal and for the good company. Please nourish it to our bodies and keep us safe through the night."

Hope took several bites. "This is really good."

"You're just saying that."

She laughed. "No, I mean it. It's delicious, Andrew." She took several more bites.

Why did his heart leap when she smiled or laughed? Almost from the moment he'd met her, they'd been running from the threat of certain death. Though the danger was still out there, this was the closest they'd come to a reprieve. Ever since his wife's death, he hadn't felt drawn to a woman until now. He'd married Helen right out of high school and she had died in a car accident only three years into their marriage. His response to the grief was to throw himself into his work and brush off any woman who hinted at a romantic interest in him. The loss had just been too devastating for him to consider loving another woman.

After they finished, they washed the few

dishes and pans together, standing side by side at the sink. She dried the last dish and turned to face him. A faint smile graced her face.

"You have some chili sauce on your face." Without thinking, he reached up and brushed his fingers over the area on the side of her mouth.

She took a step back just as color rose up in her cheeks.

He hadn't meant for the moment to become awkward.

She looked back toward the bookshelf. "Not much to do for entertainment but read," she said.

She'd broken the connection between them. Probably wise.

Entertaining thoughts about there being anything between them was pointless. As soon as the source of the leak was discovered, Hope would be whisked into a new life far from here and far from him. He didn't have to act on his feelings of attraction. He wasn't even sure if he was ready to love again.

While she moved back toward the chair by the bed, he checked his phone. A text from Valdez said the car was on the way and that he had obtained a gun for him. Andrew stepped across the floor and studied the scant selection of books on the shelf, finding one about WWII. He repositioned the couch, so he had a view out the front windows. Though he opened the book and his eyes scanned the page, much of the content was lost on him. Most of his attention was on how he was going to keep Hope safe.

The sky had begun to turn dusky. He heard the crunch of tires on gravel. Andrew shot to his feet and moved toward the window. Two cars were coming toward the cabin.

Hope stood as well. An older man with perfect posture and a little bit of a paunch got out of one of the cars and a woman pushed open the door of the other. She was easily six feet tall with her blond hair drawn up in a tight bun. Neither one of them was Agent Valdez, but they both had the undefined demeanor that gave them away as FBI agents. Still he didn't know for sure.

"Stay inside, Hope," he said.

"I might be able to help. You don't even have a gun." She moved toward the door.

He held a hand up. "I'll take care of this."

She squared her shoulders. "Haven't I proven myself?"

It was the first time she had resisted an order. "Please, let me do my job." As he stepped outside, he noted the hardness of the agent's expression.

"I'm Agent Julie Fields." The woman came toward him and held a set of keys out to him and handed him a gun in a shoulder holster. "We got a loaner car for you, sir. Valdez said you were protecting a witness. Wish we could help out but we both have to get back to Bozeman for a late briefing on an upcoming court hearing."

He took the keys. "Thanks for the car and the gun."

The agents got into the first car and drove away as he put the holster holding the gun on. Andrew checked his phone. A call had come in from an unfamiliar number, but he hadn't heard his phone ring. Reception in the cabin must be bad. Even outside, he only had two bars.

He dialed the unfamiliar number. It rang once and dropped. He stared at his phone.

The man who had been fishing was walking toward Andrew. He held a line with two fish on it. "Reception is bad out here," he said as he approached him. "For some reason, the closer you get to lake the more likely the call will go through."

"Thank you," Andrew murmured.

He stepped inside to let Hope know where he was going and why.

"Are you sure the number isn't just someone telling you your car warranty has expired?"

He laughed. Her sense of humor was endearing, and he was glad she'd gotten over being mad at him for making her stay inside. She was right that she had proved herself. "I gotta follow every lead. There is part of me wondering if this is our assassin playing games. Not sure how he would have found out my number. If he did, it means he has more tools at his disposal than I realized."

"Won't he be able to find us if he knows our number?"

"Not right away. We can just ditch this phone if we have to. The FBI might be able to help track his movements using his phone. Lock the door behind me."

Andrew stepped outside and headed toward the lake. He looked at his phone in the waning light. Sure enough, he had three bars. He hit the call back button.

He was surprised when he heard Bryson's frantic voice. "Andrew, glad you called back. I'm concerned that someone might have hacked into my cell. Got a different phone. I need to meet with you in person. I'm headed toward the airport now."

"Did you find out something?"

"I'm not sure how to interpret what I found out. Give me a second to pull over."

Andrew listened to the sound of a turn signal and then Bryson's voice came through the speaker on the phone. "As discreet as I was trying to be, someone doesn't like me snooping around."

"How do you know that?" He sucked in a breath through his teeth and braced for the answer.

"Today while I was at work, the elevator I was in was stopped. Someone threw in a rag that was on fire from the ceiling panel. The enemies list can get pretty long when you do a job like this, but I just think it is too much a coincidence in the timing. I've stirred stuff up here."

Andrew's chest squeezed tight. His boss had been put in danger, too. "I'm sorry that happened to you. Glad you were able to get out."

"The elevator was pretty smoke filled by the time someone responded to the alarm. But I'm okay." A moment of silence fell between the two men. "I need to get out of Albuquerque and not have anyone know I've left town."

"Okay, so what is the plan?"

"I'm buying my ticket at the airport, not having administration in the marshals book it so there would be no way to track where I went. What is the nearest airport to you?"

"Bozeman, I suppose."

"Great, I'll will text you with my flight time plan once I know it. Hoping to get there before midnight. You need to find a place where we can meet that is private and secure. Make sure you're not followed."

"What have you found out?"

"I need to see you in person, so we can put the pieces together. I'll get there as fast as I can."

"Okay," Andrew said. "Stay safe."

"You, too."

Andrew hung up and stalked back up the hill toward the cabin. He knocked on the door. The curtain was pulled slightly back and then Hope slid the deadbolt and opened it.

"Well?"

"We need to go on a little road trip," he told her. "I'll explain on the way."

Hope had nothing to take from the cabin but her jacket. She had noticed some bottled water in a cupboard. She grabbed two containers. It was just starting to get dark when they climbed into the loaner car and Andrew turned the key in the ignition.

She waited until he was turned around and rolling down the gravel road. "Where are we going?"

"To Bozeman to meet my boss."

"He's coming all this way on a plane?"

"Yes, he's got to get out of town. It seems his trying to find the source of the leak made someone mad enough to try to kill him."

Her breath caught. As fear rose to the surface, she gripped the armrest.

"He couldn't say over the phone what he'd found out. He's not sure what it means." Andrew pulled out onto the two-lane road.

His phone dinged. He handed it to her. "I need

to focus on driving. That might be my boss letting me know what flight he got on."

Hope picked up the phone. The text was from Valdez.

The agents now think they may have been followed to the cabin.

Hope glanced behind her. No set of headlights glared back at her.

"What does it say?"

Her throat had gone so tight, it was hard to get the words out. "The agents who brought the car believe they might have been followed."

"Wonder how. Maybe Valdez's license plate was traced back to Bozeman and the thugs figured out he was with the Bureau there. They could have been staked outside the office." He exhaled roughly. "Zimmerman must have some inside help figuring out who Valdez was and where the office was. The Queen Bee Cartel has substantial reach and network throughout the West." Andrew adjusted his rearview mirror.

As they drove toward the interstate, several cars collected behind them, one of which passed them when it had the opportunity. Once they were on the highway, traffic was heavy enough that it would be impossible to tell if they were being tailed.

Andrew's boss texted that he was on a direct flight and would be getting in at 11:43.

It was dark by the time they reached the outskirts of Bozeman. Downtown traffic was heavy. Lots of people were sitting in the outdoor bistros. Buskers on the street, and live music spilled out of some of the open bar doors. A bookstore was brightly lit, and a theater advertised a film festival.

She hadn't even realized it was Friday night. Other people were out enjoying themselves. Something that she used to do all the time when she lived in New Mexico. Since Craig's death, nothing in her life was as carefree as a Friday night downtown with friends. She doubted that it would ever be again, even if Jason Zimmerman was caught and put out of commission.

Deep longing overtook her as she listened to the laughter and chatter of people having a good time.

"This place looks pretty lively. I'm sure we can find someplace even at midnight to meet your boss." Andrew drove for several blocks before he found a parking space on a side street where the activity was just as intense. He studied his phone. "The question is where would there be a place quiet enough for us to be able to talk and not be overheard?"

Hope watched the people walking on the street, some couples and some groups of teenagers and even some families.

He put his phone away. "I don't think I'm going to find any suitable place by searching on my phone. We'll probably have to walk around and find a location. Maybe some eatery that is open but not too busy at midnight."

"Why don't we just meet Bryson at the airport and pick him up?"

"I think his reasoning was if we had an agreed-upon place, we wouldn't bring trouble to him or he to us. If either of us have a tail, we'd be able to shake it before we met up."

Once they were out on the street, Hope found herself edging closer to Andrew. The crowds made her nervous. Being close to him made her feel safer.

Jason probably knew they had been at the cabin. He might have been watching them and followed them here.

If they hadn't left when they did, an attack would have been inevitable.

Andrew wrapped a protective arm around her and leaned close to her ear so she could hear above the buzz of the crowd. "We'll just pretend like we are a couple out for a stroll."

That's all they could do. *Pretend*. She was struck by the contrast between her life and the people she saw around her. Especially the couples that seemed to be so in love.

She studied the faces of the people as they

passed. After they had walked around for twenty minutes, she saw a sign for a parking garage. "What about that?"

"It could work. We could park and wait for him. Talking in the car would be highly secure. And arriving at separate times would be a good safety measure. Not a lot of people but not totally isolated, either."

Once they stood outside the entrance to the parking garage, he peered inside.

"It looks well lit," Hope said. "I bet by midnight it won't be as full."

"Let's give it a try." They walked back to the car and drove into the parking garage, which was only three stories high.

Andrew found a place to park on the second level. The clock on the dashboard said it was eleven o'clock.

"So now we wait."

"I imagine it will be close to midnight by the time my boss gets his rental car and drives out here." He reached for the radio. "You want to listen to some music?"

She shrugged. "What else you gonna do for an hour? We could play twenty questions."

"Twenty questions?"

"You know. An icebreaker game." She flashed a grin. "Kids play it sometimes at sleepovers and Bible camp."

"Guess I missed out. You start."

"Okay, Andrew. What is your favorite color?"

"Blue, I guess," he replied.

"Now you ask me something," she said.

He stared at the roof of the car for a second. "Favorite holiday?"

"Christmas."

They went through several more questions. Then, suddenly, Andrew sat up straighter in his seat and leaned closer to the windshield. Tension descended into the car.

"That is the second time that vehicle has gone by here," he muttered.

Andrew was much more attuned to his environment and able to split his attention between the game they were playing and staying on high alert. It must be why he was good at his job.

"Maybe he's just looking for a spot. The place is pretty full."

"I don't know…" He turned the key in the ignition. "We can't take any chances. Let's move to a different part of the parking garage. See if he shows up again."

Andrew pulled out of the parking space, circling down to the first story of the garage, but not finding a parking space. Then he pulled out onto the street, turned around and went back into the garage.

As they entered, she looked over her shoulder.

There was a car behind them. The vehicle turned off, though, the second an available space came up. Andrew drove up to the third floor, where there were more open spaces.

He parked the car and killed the lights. This part of the garage had no roof and was open to a view of the taller downtown buildings.

Andrew's phone dinged. He read the text. "Bryson's landed." He texted back. "I'm letting him know where we're at."

They sat in the dark car in silence. The tension had invaded her chest, making it hard to get a deep breath.

"Favorite color?" Andrew asked.

"Anything bright. Pink, yellow, blue." Though she appreciated that he was trying to keep her distracted, her focus was no longer on the game, but on the danger that they faced.

"Your turn."

Her mind drew a blank. "First love?" The question had just spilled out.

"That's easy. My high school sweetheart who became my wife."

Andrew wasn't wearing a wedding band. She wondered what had happened.

"She died in a car wreck." His voice faltered.

Andrew had an uncanny ability to know what she was thinking.

The intensity of the emotion in his voice was

like a punch to her gut. Just like her, he had suffered intense loss. She admired him even more that he remained a man of integrity and faith. Silence fell between them as it took her a moment to respond.

"I'm sorry, Andrew. This game was meant to be fun. That was just one of the questions that girls at sleepovers ask."

He shook his head. "I'm glad that I was able to tell you." His eyes locked onto hers as a moment of connection hovered between them.

The moment was broken by his phone dinging. Andrew looked at it as his jaw went tight. "He's about five minutes away."

Hope said a quick prayer that whatever Bryson had found out would bring some resolution to who was behind the decision to hunt her down and kill her.

TEN

The sound of an approaching car made Andrew's breath catch, but the car eased by them. He hadn't asked his supervisor what he would be driving.

"He should have been here by now. I wonder what's going on." The smart thing to do would be to stay put until they heard from Bryson.

His phone dinged.

Second floor. Space E-5. You come to me. Tan compact.

Andrew relayed the information to Hope, then backed out of the space and headed down the ramp to the second story. He let the car idle while he dialed the number the text had come from.

It occurred to him that anyone could have gotten Bryson's phone and texted. A text meant you remained anonymous. He needed to hear his friend's voice to confirm they weren't being set up. He dialed the number.

"Yes."

Even with a one-word answer, he recognized Bryson's voice. "Needed to make sure it was you."

"Good call, we get too used to texting and assuming."

"We'll be there in just a minute. We are in a white SUV." Andrew pulled ahead and circled down to the second floor.

Hope watched where the numbers and letters were painted on the wall. "We just passed section D."

Andrew slowed down. As they rolled by, he saw a man sitting behind the wheel of a compact car wave at them. He couldn't see the man's face. The sign above the car said it was section E-5.

In the narrow space between his car and the parked cars, a motorcycle slipped through. As it whizzed past Bryson's car, the driver pulled a gun and shot three times at the windshield.

Andrew's heart stuttered as he pushed open the car door, reaching for his gun. The tan car's door opened as well. Bryson stumbled out. Andrew left the car running and the door ajar to get to him as Bryson stepped out onto the ramp, clutching his chest.

Andrew reached his friend just before he fell. Holding Bryson up, Andrew dragged him back to the SUV. Hope had slipped behind the wheel.

Pushing Bryson in first, Andrew got into the back seat.

"Let's get out of here," he commanded. "That motorcyclist might be coming back for round two."

Hope had already shifted and was rolling forward. Andrew turned his attention to the other man. It appeared that a bullet had entered his shoulder area. Bryson's eyes were open but unfocused. His breathing was garbled.

"We need to get him to a hospital." He touched Bryson's face. "Hang in there."

A second of recognition flashed through Bryson's eyes before he lost consciousness.

"There, I see a sign for the hospital." Hope wove expertly through the traffic of Main Street, turning onto Highland Boulevard.

The hospital came into view and she pulled up to the ER entrance. Before she'd come to a full stop, Andrew jumped out and alerted medical personnel, who came out to the car with a rolling stretcher. After lifting a still unconscious Bryson to the stretcher, they wheeled him inside.

"Why don't you go inside," Hope urged. "I'll find a place to park."

He clasped her shoulder from the back seat. "I'll stay with you. We'll go in together. Safer that way."

It would have been easy enough for the shooter on the motorcycle to follow them here or even to arrive ahead of time knowing that this would be where they would take a man who had a gunshot wound.

Hope found a parking space. Andrew got out, and they walked together toward the ER entrance. Once inside, Andrew walked to the front counter. "I'd like to know the status of the man with the gunshot wound who was just brought in. I'm not a relative. He's from out of town and doesn't know anyone here."

The woman sitting behind the counter picked up the phone. "Do you know what's happening with the GSW they just brought in? Okay, thank you." She hung up the phone and looked at Andrew. "They took him in for surgery right away. I'll let you know if there is any change."

Only one other person was in the waiting room for ER, an older woman with a walker.

Andrew sat down beside Hope. The reality of what had just happened to a man who wasn't just a work colleague but someone he cared about hit him like a blow to the stomach. He leaned forward, resting his elbows on his knees.

Hope rubbed his back. "I know. It knocks the wind out of you."

Of course, she understood; she'd witnessed her brother's death. Bryson still had a chance, but she knew what he was going through. He had so appreciated the deep empathy from her when he had told her about losing his wife. He wasn't a man who wore his heart on his sleeve, but Hope had a way of making him want to share the deeper, more painful parts of his life.

"Seeing him unconscious like that…" Andrew shook his head. "It was hard to watch."

A nurse came and got the older woman with the walker, leaving them alone in the waiting room with the receptionist. Andrew stared down at his shirt, stained with blood from where he had held Bryson.

Hope scooted closer to him touching his arm. "Do you want to pray for Bryson?"

He nodded and bowed his head but could not form the words.

Hope whispered. "Lord, we pray for Bryson to pull through and for the doctors and nurses who are trying to save him."

Her soft voice was a comfort to him.

An hour went by. Hope got them both bottled waters from a vending machine. He had just finished his water when the receptionist hung up the phone and looked in their direction. A man in scrubs came through the swinging ER door and approached them.

Even before Andrew rose to his feet and stepped toward the doctor, he knew the news wasn't good.

"We did everything we could. He just lost too much blood," the surgeon said. "I'm so sorry."

Hope touched his back gently and stepped closer to him. Her show of support was the only thing that kept his knees from buckling. His friend was dead.

"Since this was a gunshot wound, a police officer will be by to ask you some questions," the doctor told them.

Bryson had come here for a reason—he had information important enough to deliver in person. Andrew grabbed the surgeon's elbow. He pulled out his marshal ID. "If you don't mind, I think this will be handled internally."

The man nodded.

"I would like to see all his personal effects. If he had any papers with him. My boss was shot because of an ongoing investigation."

"Sure, we can do that," the surgeon replied.

Andrew could feel the surreal fog of grief descending as the receptionist handed him a clipboard and said something about his friend's body and the need to notify next of kin. Bryson had been divorced for many years and had never mentioned having children. "I think he has a sister in Santa Fe. I can call someone who would know how to contact her." One of the other marshals might know how to get in touch with the sister. Andrew had lost his original phone with his contacts but there were numbers he had committed to memory as part of his job.

He stared at the clipboard, watching the letters go in and out of focus.

Hope led him back toward the chairs. "Why don't we sit down and catch our breath."

She pulled the clipboard from his hand and set it on a chair.

"It doesn't seem real," Andrew choked out. "He was a good guy."

"I got the impression that you two were pretty close," she said gently.

"Yes, for sure. When I first joined the marshals, he was the guy who took me under his wing." Andrew swallowed hard. "We did a fishing trip together every year."

Hope's compassion was the only thing sustaining him through the searing pain of his boss's death. Her touch as she rubbed his back grounded him.

Andrew completed the paperwork and called his friend who might have the name and number of Bryson's sister. He called the sister. Though she was crying, she promised to make the arrangements for the funeral and transport of the body.

An orderly brought a bag filled with Bryson's personal effects. "We need to find someplace private. See if I can make sense of anything that Bryson brought with him. I hope that what he knew or was trying to figure out wasn't just in his head." He paced for a moment and let out a heavy breath. "Let me call Valdez, see if he can provide us with a secure space."

"It's really late," she reminded him. "Is he still going to be around?"

"Hopefully, when he sees the number, he'll pick up even if he is off duty." Andrew dialed the number and left a voice mail. "Valdez, it's Andrew. I'm in a tight spot. I wonder if you could help me out. We're in Bozeman."

They sat back down in the waiting room, which had high windows that looked out on the parking lot.

Hope paced and then sat down beside him. "Do we just wait until he calls us back?"

"We're relatively safe inside the hospital. Once we go outside, I have to assume that the same man who came after Bryson will come for us."

"Guess it would be pretty easy for him to figure out that we went to the hospital." Her voice dropped half an octave. "He's probably waiting for us out there."

"That's the assumption we have to operate on," he said. Still struggling with losing Bryson, Andrew vowed that no one else would die on his watch.

A chill ran down Hope's back as she stared out at the rows of cars lit by the streetlamps. A motorcycle could be tucked away anywhere. The assassin might not be able to locate their car, but he could watch the entrances for them. She wondered, too, if the man on the motorcycle was the same one who had been with Jason.

This time of night, the ER might be the only entrance that was even open. They couldn't hope to sneak out some other way.

Andrew shifted in the seat beside her. His shoulder brushed against hers. He was clearly torn apart by Bryson's death and she wished she could offer deeper comfort to him, to take the pain away. Though she had not known Bryson, she was so connected to Andrew that she felt a chasm from the loss as well.

She let out a breath when Andrew's phone rang. As she listened to one side of the conversation, it sounded like Valdez would send someone to help them.

Andrew finished up the conversation. "Okay, tell her to look for us just inside the ER waiting room. We should be able to see her coming." He clicked the disconnect button. "The female agent who dropped off the car is available to escort us to a Bureau office."

While they waited, several people came into the waiting room. A man pressed a hand over a bleeding cut on his forehead. Then she watched an overwrought mother holding a listless child in her arms. Within ten minutes, a tall blond woman dressed in workout gear made her way toward the waiting room entrance. He recognized her as Agent Julie Fields, the woman who had dropped off the car.

They both rose at the same time as the woman stepped into the interior of the hospital.

She held a hand out to Andrew. "Valdez said you guys ran into more trouble."

"To say the least." Andrew shook her hand and then turned toward Hope. "This is Hope Miller. The witness I've been assigned to protect."

Agent Fields shook her hand as well.

They stepped out into the cool, dark night.

Walking a few paces in front of them, Agent Fields looked over her shoulder. "Where are you parked?"

"Third row, about five cars in," Hope said.

"Why don't I bring my car around to you." Agent Fields kept walking while she talked. "You should make sure your vehicle is secure."

Hope wondered what she meant by *secure*. Looking for bombs or if someone was in the back seat maybe?

The notion made her shudder.

As they approached their borrowed car, another car started up somewhere in the lot. Andrew glanced around. "Hope, why don't you stand by that light pole while I check the car out."

He dropped to his knees and peered underneath the car.

The night chill sank into her skin as Andrew searched the front and back seats, then popped the hood.

A car rolled toward them from the far end of the lot.

Hope stiffened for a moment until she saw Agent Fields's blond hair. The female agent let the car idle while Andrew looked in the trunk.

"All clear," he said.

They got into the car. Andrew checked the mirror waiting for Agent Fields to pull forward before backing out and following the other car through the lot and onto the street.

They wove through several streets where homes and businesses had dark windows before coming back out on a wide main thoroughfare where there were hotels, restaurants and retail stores.

Agent Fields seemed to be taking the scenic route to wherever she was leading them.

Andrew's tense glances in the mirrors must be him making sure they were not being followed.

The motorcycle came out of nowhere. It was suddenly beside them on the driver's side.

In an instant, the driver had raised a handgun and aimed while Andrew jerked the wheel and veered over the divider. Turning to avoid the car coming toward him, he ended up on the sidewalk. A single shot had been fired. Hope wasn't sure where the bullet had gone.

On the street up ahead, Agent Fields had pulled over.

Andrew looked in all directions as he reached out to touch Hope's forearm. "You okay?"

She couldn't see the motorcycle anywhere, but that didn't mean he couldn't turn around and come back for them again. "I'm not hit." Her heart pounded as she struggled to respond. "Just kind of shaken."

He squeezed her hand and patted her shoulder. "Understandable."

Andrew waited for a car to pass, then turned around in the street and back over to where Agent Fields waited for them. He pulled in behind her.

The FBI agent got out and Andrew rolled down the window. Behind him, he could see that several police cars had come to the place where the shooting and consequent accident had happened.

Agent Fields leaned in. "A little too much excitement there, huh?"

"More than I needed tonight," Andrew replied gruffly.

"I already let the local cops know that the accident was a matter the Bureau was dealing with, so they won't need to question you." Agent Fields lifted her head and stared out on the street. "I was going to take you to a field office and open it up for you, but I think you better follow me to my place." She recited the address and Andrew put it in his phone. "I think you need a little extra protection. Stay close. I might have to take some detours if I think that we're being tailed."

"Got it," he said.

Hope watched the red taillights of the agent's car as they wove through city streets and then residential neighborhoods, finally coming to what appeared to be the end of town where the houses were on large lots on hills. They took a winding road to a colonial-style house with an attached garage.

The garage door came open and Agent Fields's car disappeared inside.

She and Andrew waited in the car until a light went on above the front door, and the agent ushered them in. Andrew remained close to her as they made their way up the stone walkway.

Once inside, Hope turned to look through the big front windows, which gave a view of the twinkling lights of the city below.

Agent Fields headed toward the stairs. "There's a guest room on this floor and a couch. Let me grab some blankets."

Hope clicked on the light by the couch and collapsed. Andrew sat down beside her, looking overwhelmed. He clutched the bag that contained Bryson's belongings.

Agent Fields returned with blankets and pillows, which she sat on the spare cushion on the couch. "Help yourself to anything in the kitchen. Guest room is just over there."

Whether it was numbness over what had happened to Bryson or exhaustion, Hope was having a hard time responding.

Andrew shifted in his seat. "Thanks for everything."

"We'll get this straightened out in the morning. I have a teenage son who is away at a tournament. Otherwise I wouldn't have brought you here and risked his safety." She cupped Hope's shoulder. "I'll just be upstairs, and I'm armed. My husband is not law enforcement, but he knows how to use a gun as well."

Hope nodded. "I just pray we haven't brought trouble to your door."

"I can handle it," the agent assured her. She turned and went up the stairs.

Both of them sat in the near darkness for a long moment. Upstairs, they heard someone moving around and then the house fell silent.

Hope rose to her feet. Andrew had a glazed look in his eyes. "Not sure I can go to sleep just yet. Why don't I get us both a glass of water or a cup of tea or something."

She entered the kitchen and turned on the light. It took only a moment to find mugs and tea bags. Andrew came and sat down at the kitchen table. He placed the bag that contained his colleague's personal items on the table and rested his hand on it.

"I think we should look through this stuff," he said. "Maybe it will tell us who the leak is."

She opened a tea bag and placed it in the mug she'd filled with water. "Do you feel ready to do that?"

"It's not a matter of me feeling ready. The clock is ticking. It's just a matter of time before there is another attempt on your life. The priority needs to be with getting this resolved so you can enter into a safe and secure life without fear that this will happen again."

She put the first mug in the microwave and pushed the button to heat the water.

Hope sat down beside Andrew and placed her hand on his. He was thinking more of her than himself and his grief over losing Bryson. "If you're sure. I know you're torn up over his death...."

He met her gaze. She saw a quiet strength there that calmed her troubled mind.

He let out a labored breath. "It's a lot to deal with, but no more than you have been through.

The last few hours have been pretty harrowing for you."

Her hand still covered his. She squeezed his fingers. "I'm just glad you were here with me."

"I'm glad you're okay." His unwavering gaze drew her in.

The microwave dinged, breaking up the moment between them. She pushed her chair back, pulled the mug out and put the other one in. Hope sat the cup down beside Andrew and touched his shoulder. "Whenever you're ready."

He stared at the bag.

Would they find anything that would explain the reason Bryson had come all this way, only to lose his life in the process?

ELEVEN

Andrew reached for the bag that held his boss's possessions. After Hope put second cup of tea in the microwave, she sat kitty-corner from him at the table.

He pulled out Bryson's keys, a watch and a wallet, as well as several small pieces of paper. Seeing each item caused a stab to his heart.

Andrew shook his head when he saw the pieces of paper. One was a Post-it and another looked like it had been torn from a small note-book. "This is Bryson's version of case notes. Most of what he had concluded was probably in his head." Andrew's chest squeezed tight when he saw several dots of blood on the scrap paper.

Hope scooted her chair closer and patted his upper arm.

The scrap of paper was a list of four names. The Post-it had a doodle of a bumblebee, Hope and her brother Craig's name with question marks and an arrow pointing to the doodle of the bee. "These must be people within WITSEC that Bryson was suspicious of for whatever reason." He pointed to the third name. "I recognize this name. She's the caseworker who put together your new identity." Then he gestured to the second name. "This guy is a marshal who just transferred to the New Mexico District."

"The caseworker would have known everything about the new me," Hope said.

"Yes, other people might have helped with parts of getting you set up, but she would have had the whole picture in front of her." He tapped the piece of paper. "My gut feeling is that she is also the least likely person."

"Why do you say that? Because she's the most obvious? She wouldn't have to go dig for any information on me."

"She's been there a long time and handled tons of cases. Unless someone else was threatening her or had some leverage against her, I just don't think she would be the most likely suspect."

"Okay, so that leaves three others."

Andrew stared at the other names. "I don't know enough about this new marshal and I don't recognize the other two names. They must be pencil pushers on the administrative side of the program."

The microwave dinged and Hope rose to get her cup of tea. Andrew took a sip of the minty liquid and looked at the other piece of paper. Bryson had clearly been thinking about the Queen Bee Cartel in relationship to Craig. He took in a breath knowing the questions he had to ask Hope might be painful and intrusive, though she had shared some details already. "If it wasn't a drug debt that your brother was killed over, what was it?"

She sat back down and took a long moment to blow on her tea. "I don't know."

"It didn't make sense to me to send the number two guy to kill Craig just for a drug debt, and Jason Zimmerman kept asking you questions about your brother's things. There might be something deeper going on."

"Well, I got the impression Jason was going to kill me whether I told him or not. Maybe he got paid extra if he found out." She took a sip. "I thought maybe my brother had something they wanted back, like maybe they were mad because he took some of their drugs and was going to turn it in to the police."

"But the police would have found something like that when they went over the crime scene. It must be something else that wouldn't put off alarm bells to law enforcement."

Hope wrapped her hands around the mug. "I have no idea what that would be."

"Where are your brother's things?"

Her jaw went slack, and she stared at the wall for a moment. "Everything happened so fast. Once the police knew I could testify against Lincoln Kramer, I was put in a safe house." Her voice faltered. "I couldn't even go to Craig's funeral." She let out a sob as her hand went to her mouth. She shook her head, tears glistening in her eyes.

His heart lurched as he covered her hand to comfort her. "I know this is a lot to have to relive." He hated putting her through this.

She swiped at her eyes. "It's okay. Thinking about this is the only way to get Jason and the people who hired him. I don't want them to win. It would mean Craig's death was for nothing."

He admired her quiet strength so much.

She sat up straighter and lifted her chin. "Now that I think about it, our godfather Lawrence might have been the one to get Craig's stuff. He owns some land and would have had a place to store my brother's items. He might have cleaned out my stuff, too. That's the kind of thing he would have done." She took a sip of the tea and put the cup down. "I guess I thought I would be able to get my things at some point. That is the unreality of being put into the program."

Andrew looked at the drawing again. "You had never heard of the Queen Bee Cartel before Craig's death?"

She shook her head. "We lived very different lives, my brother and I."

"We can't just storm into the WITSEC offices in New Mexico and start asking questions. We'd be killed for sure. I wonder if there is some way we could get access to your brother's things."

"I won't put my godfather in danger," she insisted. "Chances are we would be followed if we went back to New Mexico."

"Understood. But I wonder if we can arrange for the stuff to be brought somewhere so we can look through it."

"Maybe. I'd have to look up Lawrence's number," she said. "I don't have it memorized."

"Soon as we have some daylight, we should do that." He took another drink of tea. "I don't know about you, but I feel like I can sleep now. You can have the guest bedroom."

Hope rose to her feet and gathered the almost empty mugs to put in the sink. "Yeah, I guess I should try to get some sleep as well."

She stepped back into the living room and he followed. She turned to face him at the guest room door. "What if there is nothing in my brother's stuff?"

"I'm not sure what we'd do, then. I hope it's not a dead end."

"Me, too." Hope reached out and squeezed his shoulder.

She disappeared into the guest room as the warmth of her touch faded from his skin. Andrew tossed a pillow toward the end of the couch and unfolded one of the blankets Julie had brought down. He sat on the couch for a long moment watching the glittery lights of the city below.

This house appeared to be on a cul-de-sac with three other houses. Any car coming up here in the darkness would draw attention to itself. That didn't mean the assassin couldn't park below and approach on foot. A motorcycle would be even easier to hide.

After kicking off his shoes, he lay down and pulled the blanket around him knowing that he had to sleep lightly and remain vigilant.

Hope fell asleep trying to remember her god-father's phone number but knowing she'd have to do an internet search. Contacting someone from her old life held its own set of dangers. The person behind the leak was powerful enough to hire a hit man from the program. Assuming he or she had the help of the Queen Bee's resources, they might also be watching the people who had been important to her in her old life.

She thought of her best friend from work, another second-grade teacher. Adele Hozeman was set to retire at the end of this year. Images of other people who had been important in her life flashed through her mind. It was bad enough she no longer had her brother; she wasn't about to put anyone she cared about in danger.

Her eyes warmed with tears and she drifted off to sleep. She hoped she and Andrew were making the right choice.

Hours later, she woke when the sun sneaked through the closed blinds. She heard voices in the kitchen as she got up to shower. A set of clothes, a new toothbrush and a tube of toothpaste were sitting on the dresser by the door.

After she showered and changed, she heard the sound of voices in the kitchen. She found Andrew and Julie sitting at the table talking with coffee cups and empty plates in front of them.

The FBI agent rose to her feet. "I thought you might be about my size if not as tall." She pointed at the hoodie, blouse and capris that Hope had dressed in. "It's just a little big on you."

"I appreciate having some fresh clothes. Thank you for being so considerate." It looked like Andrew had borrowed some of Julie's husband's clothes. He looked handsome in the forest-colored khakis and rust-colored T-shirt.

"You look nice," she said to him.

Color rose up in his cheeks. "Thanks."

The moments of attraction seemed to happen more and more between them and yet, they were always pulled back to the present danger in their lives. The only thing that made it bearable was Andrew's comforting presence.

"Mike, my husband, has already left for the day." Julie stepped over to the counter. "Can I get you some pancakes and coffee?"

"Sure, if they're already made." Hope took a chair next to Andrew.

Julie scooped the pancakes off the griddle and put them in the microwave. "Andrew briefed me on your case. He tells me that you guys have come up with a plan to get access to the things that were in your brother's place at the time of his death."

"That's right," Andrew told the agent, then nodded toward Hope. "I was thinking you could contact your godfather and make arrangements for the stuff to be transported to a storage unit somewhere."

Julie set a coffee mug in front of Hope. Andrew pushed the sugar and half-and-half toward her before taking a sip from his own mug.

"If a moving company did the transporting, that would make it less likely that my godfather would be in harm's way."

"I have a friend in Wyoming who used to be a marshal until he got shot and had to take early retirement," Andrew said. "Now that I think about it, he has a hunting cabin that would be more secure than a storage unit. He might be able to help us. I don't know what was in your brother's place, but we don't need the furniture to be hauled, just personal stuff."

"What if there is something valuable hidden under a cushion or something? We don't know what we are looking for…if anything."

"I think the crime scene people would have done a thorough search," he replied. "It must be something that on the surface looks so innocuous they overlooked it."

Julie put the warmed-up pancakes in front of Hope, along with syrup and butter. "Let me grab my laptop, so you can at least look up your godfather's phone number."

Julie left the room.

"You look tired," Andrew murmured.

"I didn't sleep really well." After putting butter and syrup on her pancakes, Hope took a bite of her breakfast, enjoying the sweetness and warmth.

"Sorry about the rough night. I know you have a lot on your mind." His voice filled with compassion.

"Tell me about this friend of yours."

"His hunting cabin has a year-round road to it and is fairly accessible." Andrew rose to his feet to pour another cup of coffee.

"How much will all that cost to transport?"

"I'm pretty sure I can put it on the marshals' dime in the name of keeping you safe."

"But if you have to put in a request for funds, what if the wrong eyes see it and they figure out what we're planning?"

"I thought of that. Marshals are funded separate from WITSEC. We have other duties not connected to that organization."

"You said one of the names on that list was a marshal, a new guy."

"True." Andrew tapped his fingers on the table.

Julie returned with the laptop and set it on the kitchen table. She loaded the dishwasher while she talked. "The car you guys are driving belongs to the Bureau. It needs to be returned, but I can drive you to a rental place if you like."

Hope still wasn't sure how feasible this plan was.

Andrew leaned closer to her. "We can do this on my dime and then I can look to get reimbursement, if that would make you feel safer."

"That's a big sacrifice, Andrew."

"Believe me, I was thinking about this last night. If there is any other way, I would suggest that. But if I send one of my marshal friends in to poke around, they might meet with the same fate as Bryson. And I can't take that risk." A muscle ticked in his jaw. "I think trying to figure out why your brother was killed is the next logical step."

Emotion glimmered in her eyes. "The Queen

Bee Cartel wanted my brother gone for some reason."

"And we will figure out the reason. I promise you that."

Before she could respond, Julie sat down at the table and interjected, "Actually...that cartel has come up on our radar more than once. Largest distributor in the western US."

"No one knows for sure who really runs the whole operation," Andrew said. "They think it's a woman, thus the name."

Hope pulled the laptop toward her and typed in her godfather's name. Lawrence Holt had been a friend of her father's. She and Craig had spent part of the summer on his farm as kids. After a brief search, his name and number came up on the screen.

Julie grabbed a piece of paper and pen from a drawer so Hope could write down the number. "If you don't mind, I'll let you make your phone call. I need to move some sprinklers and check on the chickens in the backyard." She stepped out the kitchen door.

Andrew placed his phone in front of Hope.

"It will be good to hear Lawrence's voice again," Hope said.

Andrew pushed his chair away from the table. "Why don't we go make the call in the living room."

She rose from her chair as Andrew stepped into the living room. When she looked out the kitchen window, she saw Julie disappear behind a shed that must be where the chickens were kept.

Movement on a different part of the backyard out of the corner of her eye caught her attention and a second later, the kitchen window shattered.

She screamed.

TWELVE

At the sound of Hope's scream, Andrew whirled around just in time to see her drop to the floor as glass exploded through the kitchen. He ran to pull her to safety, dropping to his hands and knees when he entered the kitchen.

Hope had curled up and placed her arms over her head.

He wrapped his arms around her torso. "This way."

They stood up to get over the shards but remained bent at the waist. He led her back to the living room, wondering if they would even be safe there. They crouched in front of the couch. When he lifted his head, he had a view of the shattered window. Several escaped chickens wandered the yard.

"Where's Julie?"

"She was still outside," Hope told him. "I couldn't see her once she went behind that shed.

Do you think something might have happened to her?"

If Julie wasn't incapacitated, she would have run into the house for her gun by now. He turned and lifted his head to see out the living room windows that faced the road as well as the side windows.

The guy had to still be out there waiting for another chance to get a shot at Hope. He could be circling the house looking for his opportunity at a different window.

His hand touched his gun. "Go to the guest room and find a hiding place. Stay below window level."

Hope nodded and whispered for him to be careful as she crawled toward the open door of the guest room.

He surveyed the area outside. No strange cars were parked on the street. The car in the driveway was the one he'd borrowed. None were parked on the road, either. The winding road up here had had plenty of turnouts where someone could park a car or a motorcycle. The guy must have hiked in.

He checked the windows in the other rooms as well, looking for any sign of the shooter. If he was out there, he was well hidden.

Andrew moved toward the kitchen. He opened the back door quietly and stepped out onto a covered patio. Then he made his way toward the shed, where Hope said she'd last seen Julie.

Still no more shots were fired. He found Julie lying on the ground still breathing but unconscious. They would both be extremely exposed if he carried her back to the house. He'd be unable to use the gun to defend himself if he had to hold her.

He touched her cheeks lightly. "Julie, wake up. We're under assault."

She was unresponsive. He'd left his phone on the kitchen table. He wasn't sure if calling an ambulance was the best idea anyway. Andrew still wasn't sure what the shooter was up to and he didn't want to put more people in danger.

He wrapped an arm underneath Julie and lifted her to a sitting position.

She made a soft groaning noise and her eyes squeezed tighter. Her head shook. "What happened?" Her voice was faint and wavering.

"I think someone hit you in the head. We need to get back to the house. Someone took a shot at Hope through your kitchen window."

The information caused her to raise her head. "Is she all right?"

"Yes, we need to get inside and call the police just in case the guy is still around."

Maybe the shooter had taken one shot and left. Something may have scared him away. It just didn't seem likely given the tenacity with which Hope had been hunted down so far.

Julie gripped the back of her head when she

leaned forward and attempted to stand. Andrew helped her get to her feet. He supported her as they made their way to the back door. When he tried the door, it was locked.

Now he understood why another shot had not been fired. He knew that if he ran around to the front door, it would be locked as well. "Someone is in there with Hope. I've got to find a way in before it's too late."

"I'll go to the neighbors and call the police."

Julie took off across the yard at a jogging pace. She probably hadn't totally recovered from being hit on the head. The houses were so far apart up here, Andrew could not even see the neighbor's house Julie was headed toward.

He braced for the sound of a gunshot as he slammed his body against the kitchen door.

The man with a gun had a crazed look in his eyes when he glared at Hope. He wasn't Jason or the blond thug.

When she'd first heard the sound of footsteps in the house, Hope had thought it was Andrew coming back inside. But something about the intensity of the stomping had caused her not to call out his name.

There was no lock on the guest bedroom door. This intruder had found her easily enough even though she'd hidden in the closet.

Now, he stood over her, gun aimed at her heart.

She backed into a corner, her hands up in a defensive posture. "Please, don't shoot me."

Sweat ran down his face as he adjusted the gun in his hand. He spoke haltingly. "You just need to tell me where your brother's things are...and I will go. I promise."

The man in front of her was no trained killer like Jason Zimmerman. She thought she saw fear in his eyes, or maybe it was paranoia. All signs indicated he was an addict going through withdrawal. The gun shook in his hand as he licked his lips and glanced around as if someone was going to jump out at him. A man prone to erratic behavior and holding a gun was just as scary as a professional hit man.

"I don't know where his things are."

The man's finger went inside the trigger guard. "You do."

"Please, if you shoot me, you'll never find out."

The man looked sideways for a moment as if thinking about what she had said.

A repeated banging noise caused them both to jump. Someone was trying to get into the house. The doors must be locked. That man wasn't completely out of it if he had the foresight to do that.

"You're coming with me." He lunged at her.

She angled to get away but in the small space between the bed and the closet, there was nowhere to go. He grabbed her arm above the elbow, squeezing tight, pulled her forward and pressed the gun into her back.

The banging continued.

"Get going, now." He pushed the gun against her spine while ushering her into the living room toward the front door.

She remembered the broken kitchen window. If she cried out, Andrew might be able to hear her. The man might shoot her on the spot, though.

She waited until they were at the front door, and he had twisted the deadbolt and unlocked the knob. She needed to create a distraction. She doubled over and clutched her stomach. "I think I'm going to be sick."

The man withdrew the gun.

She grabbed a lamp on the entryway table and swung it at him. Crying out in pain, he bent over. She hit him again, but he didn't fall to the ground. While he recovered, she had a few seconds of delay before he could react.

She threw the lamp at his head and ran for the cover of the couch. She saw the folly in her plan. If she yelled at Andrew that the front door was open, the assailant would simply relock it.

She could hear the man stomping toward her. She scrambled to get to the back door to let Andrew in.

The gunman fired a shot, but it didn't hit her.

To not miss her, he must not have wanted to kill her, only scare her, or his hand was so shaky his aim wasn't accurate even at this close range.

He caught her just as she stepped across the threshold and yelled Andrew's name. The banging stopped for a moment.

The man slammed against the wall and put the gun under her chin.

Now she saw rage in his eyes. "You tried to get away from me."

His sudden emotional shifts reinforced her belief that he was on some kind of drug.

Andrew was at the broken window, gun aimed. The man's back was to the window, but Hope could see Andrew over her attacker's shoulder. If Andrew shot the man, he'd risked shooting Hope, too.

The man grabbed her arm and swung her around. She had a brief moment when she saw Andrew, but the thug's back was still to the window. She mouthed the words *front door*.

"All you got to do is tell me where your brother's things are." He pushed her into the living room. "That's all I need from you, lady."

They were ten feet from the front door.

She slowed her steps.

The door burst open.

Andrew entered with his gun drawn. "Let her go."

The man placed his pistol on Hope's heart. He

was shaking so badly she could feel the vibrations through the barrel.

"The police will be here any minute," Andrew warned him. "Let her go and this will all go more smoothly for you."

"You didn't call the police. You didn't have a phone."

Andrew kept his aim steady. "The lady who lives here ran to the neighbors."

The barrel of the gun shook even worse. She couldn't see if her attacker's finger was on the trigger or not. If so, there was a huge danger of the gun going off accidentally.

"I don't believe you," the man said. His free hand went to the back of Hope's neck. He was close enough to her that she could hear his shallow, uneven breathing and smell his sweat.

"Put the gun down and step away from her." Andrew's voice remained strong and authoritative.

She feared that the arrival of police might set this deranged man off and make him not care what happened. They had to disarm him before then.

"Please," she said. "I can see you're not a killer."

"I got debts that need to be paid." His voice held a note of anguish.

Andrew shook his head. "This isn't the way to do this. Put the gun down."

The pressure on her chest let up slightly, and

she thought he was going to toss the gun. Instead, the man moved it to her head so he could step behind her and use her as a shield. He pulled her backward.

Andrew took a step closer.

"Take a shot. Maybe you'll hit her and maybe you'll hit me." The man's voice had become stronger as he tugged on her shirt and they walked backward toward the kitchen door.

He glanced over his shoulder and then looked back at Andrew, who kept his gun up and took another step into the living room. His expression gave away his frustration.

The man kept backing up. They stepped across the kitchen threshold.

She heard the sirens in the distance.

Without warning, the man pushed her to the floor. Three shots were fired. The gunfire seemed to echo through the house. She had no idea who had fired. She crawled toward the kitchen table and placed her hands over her head.

She had a view of the man's feet as he unlocked the back door, opened it and fled.

When she peered in the living room. She didn't see Andrew.

She called out his name.

Had he been shot?

THIRTEEN

From where he'd taken cover in front of the couch, Andrew barely heard Hope's cry as the sirens grew louder. He'd managed to fire one shot once the assailant had stepped clear of Hope. Two shots had gone off from the other man's gun.

"Hope, I'm okay." He stuck his head above the couch but couldn't see her.

The cops pounded on the front door. "Police, open up."

Andrew rose and walked toward the door. "I'll open the door slowly. I'm not the guy you're looking for." After pulling the door open, he held his hands up in a surrender pose. "I'm a US marshal. The man you're after ran out the back door."

Two officers stood on the front porch, an older man and a younger one. The one closest to the door, the man with gray hair, responded, "We've already sent two officers around the back, standard procedure."

"If you don't mind. The woman who was held hostage is in the kitchen. I know you will want to talk to us, but I need to go to her and make sure she's okay."

The officer nodded.

Before he turned away, he caught a glimpse of Julie standing at the end of the driveway. She'd gone beyond the call of duty and now she had to deal with a damaged house.

Andrew hurried into the kitchen. Hope was sitting in a kitchen chair with a dazed look on her face.

He reached down and gathered her into his arms, stroking her hair and repeating, "It's okay. You're all right now."

Through the broken kitchen window, he watched the two officers cuff the man who had come after Hope and lead him away.

Maybe the guy would have information about who had hired him, but he was clearly just an addict probably trying to pay off some debt or score more drugs.

He held Hope for a long moment until she pulled away.

"I'll get you a glass of water," he said

She nodded but the look in her eyes told him she was still in shock. He moved to the kitchen sink and turned on the water. Then he placed the glass in front of her and took a chair close to her.

She shook her head in disbelief. "We have to find a way to end this."

The younger officer poked his head in the kitchen. "We've got the man in custody. We're going to need to ask you some questions."

"Why don't you start with me?" Julie had stepped into the living room. "Andrew can make sure Hope is okay."

Julie gave a brief summary the younger officer about what had transpired. The younger officer looked at Julie. "You received a blow to the head. Don't you think you should be checked out medically?"

Julie touched the back of her head. "I'll be okay?"

"It's your call." The officer looked at her face more closely. "Your pupils aren't dilated."

The younger officer then sat at the table with Hope and Andrew. His questions were posed in a gentle way, so Hope was able to explain what had happened.

Once the officers left, Julie sat down at the kitchen table with Andrew and Hope. She stared at the broken glass on the kitchen floor. There were probably bullet holes in the walls as well.

"Looks like I will have quite a story to tell Mike when he gets home," Julie remarked.

"This was above and beyond giving us some

help. I'm sure the Marshals Service will foot the bill for the repair."

"We'll get it worked out," she replied.

Hope took a sip of her water. She still stared at the floor. Slowly she lifted her head and made eye contact. "That guy wanted to know what I did with my brother's things. If I had any doubt that figuring out what he was killed for has to be our next move, I don't anymore."

The piece of paper that had her godfather's phone number on it had fallen off the kitchen table. Andrew rose from his chair and picked it up, setting it beside Hope.

"Let me call my friend with the hunting cabin first," he said.

Julie rose from the chair and got a broom to sweep up the broken glass. "I'm still glad to take you to the car rental place."

"We've got to act fast. I'm sure whoever is behind this will just send someone else once he or she finds out the last guy didn't succeed." He picked up his phone. "I'll call my friend."

He walked into the living room to have a private conversation. Dean Stanford picked up on the third ring.

"Hello, Dean," he said. "It's Andrew."

"Andrew, it's been a while. This isn't your old phone number."

"Long story that I can't get into right now. I'm

in the middle of escorting a witness and the whole thing has gone sideways. I'm sure you're up on the Lincoln Kramer trial."

"Yeah, the high-ranking guy in the Queen Bee Cartel. You're escorting that witness?"

"That's right. It looks like the cartel got someone in WITSEC to turn over her relocation info. In addition to wanting her dead for revenge, we think they are after something that was in her brother's place when he was shot. We need to have the stuff brought somewhere not likely to be breached or discovered. I thought your hunting cabin might work."

"Sure, not a problem. Anything to help," Dean said. "It'll be good to see you."

"Great, when we figure out the logistics, I'll give you a call back."

Andrew hung up and returned to the kitchen. Julie was back outside gathering runaway chickens into the coop. He set the phone down beside Hope and squeezed her shoulder. "Whenever you're ready you can call your godfather."

Hope read the phone number and touched the keypad on the phone. Her voice quavered as she spoke. "Hey, Lawrence, this is Hope. I know you probably thought you'd never hear from me again... Yes, it's good to hear your voice, too." Her eyes rimmed with tears.

Andrew covered her hand that wasn't holding the phone with his own. He knew being reminded of the life she had lost would not be easy.

"Listen, I have a big favor to ask of you. Did you pack up the things from Craig's apartment and put them in your barn?"

Hope was silent while Lawrence talked.

"So there's only eight or so boxes of personal stuff?"

They talked for a little while longer, and she finished up the phone call telling Lawrence they would be in touch once they had made arrangements for the movers to come. After an emotional goodbye, she hung up.

Julie had come back in the house with a basket that had half a dozen eggs in it, which she placed in the refrigerator.

Andrew made several calls to movers in Santa Fe before he found one that could get Craig's belongings as soon as possible. As it was, it would take two days for the stuff to be picked up and delivered to the cabin in Wyoming. The drive for them would only take a day, even though Santa Fe and Bozeman were about the same distance to where the cabin was outside Cheyenne.

He called his friend back to let him know about the timeline they had set up. Although he wasn't sure where they would go while they waited for the stuff to arrive at the cabin, he only knew they needed to get out of Bozeman.

He didn't want to put Julie and her family at any further risk.

Once they were ready, they got into the agent's car so she could drive them to the car rental place.

At the bottom of the hill where the subdivision connected with a main road, Andrew noticed a car pull off a shoulder where it had been parked and slip in behind them.

"I think we're being followed," he said.

Hope tensed as she looked out the rear window from the back seat where she sat. Though it hung back, the other car was the only other one on the road. A sense of dread invaded her awareness. She still wasn't over the attack at Julie's house. The man had been so erratic and unpredictable. It was as if she had to relive the violence of Craig's death all over again.

Julie glanced in the rearview mirror. "It seems to me like he was waiting at the bottom of the hill. We can't take any chances. I'll take the scenic route to the car rental place."

She wove through city streets before taking an exit that led to the airport.

Though Hope did not see the indistinct dark sedan as they pulled into the car rental place, she didn't discount that it was still around. It was an automobile that blended in easily.

Julie got out of the car with them and hugged

them both. "Praying everything goes smoothly for you."

"Thanks for everything," Andrew said.

Hope stayed close to him as they walked into the car rental place. Through the large windows, she saw airplanes landing and taking off. Julie waved at her before she backed her car up. The woman would be going back to her home and family.

It had been gut-wrenching to talk to Lawrence and be reminded of her old life. She prayed that the reach of whoever was behind this did not extend to watching her godfather's place or harming him in any way. The plan they had was less than perfect.

Andrew filled out the paperwork for the rental car, and they stepped outside to find it on the lot. Once they found the car, a blue SUV, they got in with Andrew in the driver's seat.

"What now?"

"We get as far away from Bozeman as we can. It will take two days for that stuff to be delivered. I don't want to be hanging around the cabin before it gets there. Too much of a chance we'll be found and ambushed. And if we don't go directly to the cabin, we have a better chance of shaking any tail we might have."

Andrew drove back out to the highway. The miles and the small towns clipped by. She noticed that he checked his mirrors from time to time. Traffic was heavy enough that someone tailing them could hang back and not be noticed.

They crossed the state line into Wyoming.

His vigilance caused a knot of tension to form at the back of her neck. "Maybe we need to find a place to hide out."

"I'm sure there are lots of hiding places in Wyoming." He let out a heavy sigh.

She saw the weariness in his expression. "This is way more than you counted on when you picked me up to be taken to Whitetail."

"As a marshal, my job is to make sure the witness is kept safe from the forces that could harm him or her." He glanced at her and smiled. "Sometimes that duty just gets a little more complicated."

His smile seemed a little forced. "I'm just sorry to put you through this. But also incredibly grateful that it was you who was the one to escort me. You clearly know what you are doing when it comes to protecting a witness."

In response, he gave her a smile that was much more genuine. A little color rose up in his cheeks. "Well, thank you."

She could feel the heat in her own face. Embarrassed, she turned to stare out the window at the forest that butted up against the highway. The moment of connection had lifted her spirits, but she knew nothing could come of it. Even if he was her contact person once she got a new identity, being involved with him would be impossible and put them both in danger. For that reason, he probably wouldn't remain her contact person. Andrew may has well have been living on Mars.

Besides, she didn't even know if the attraction was real or just because he was so kind and protective and the only thing she had to cling to that was stable. Deciding you had feelings for someone in the midst of this kind of turmoil seemed foolhardy.

Andrew spoke up. "At the next small town, we'll stop and get a bite to eat."

It was late afternoon, and breakfast had been a long time ago. In some ways, the quiet morning before all the trouble had been a lifetime ago. She shuddered when she thought of the desperate, glassy-eyed man who had held a gun against her chest.

The sign on the highway advertised that the next town had two fast-food places they could eat at.

Andrew hit the blinker and took the exit. "Chicken or tacos?"

"Chicken, I guess," she said.

Once they were in town, both fast-food outlets as well as a gas station were visible. She saw several rows of older-looking houses up the road.

Andrew parked in front of the chicken place, where there was only one other car in the lot. "Wish this place had a drive-through. That would be a lot safer."

They walked up to the counter and put in an order. The lunch hour had passed. A group of four girls giggling at a table sipping drinks and a single man dressed in work clothes were the only other occupants in the place.

All the same, Andrew's posture, the squared shoulders and the lifted chin, suggested a state of high alert. He was right not to let his guard down and she couldn't, either. They had been attacked too many times to assume they had managed to shake the forces that wanted her dead.

FOURTEEN

Andrew sat so he had a view of the street and the car.

The chicken, biscuits and coleslaw were a salve to his empty stomach. They had almost completed the meal when a motorcycle rolled by on the street. The driver wore a helmet that covered his face, but he appeared to be looking at the rental car and going slower than required.

Andrew did not want to alarm Hope. They had never gotten a clear look at the type of motorcycle the assassin who killed Bryson had been on. He wondered, too, if the assassin was the same blond man they had seen in Whitetail with Jason.

He simply could not take any chances.

Andrew burst to his feet. "We should get going."

Hope stared down at her half-eaten meal. "Okay, I'll take this with me and eat it in the car."

Once they were settled in the car, she said, "I take it you saw something that was concerning."

She took a bite of her chicken and wiped her fingers on a napkin.

"Not sure, just don't want to take any chances." Andrew backed up and turned back toward the highway.

The towns in Wyoming were small and separated by rolling hills and forest. He debated if it was safer to find a place to stay in one of the towns where there were people or to get some supplies and hide out in a forested area or remote campground.

He had to make choices under the assumption they had been followed from Bozeman.

Andrew saw a sign for a town called Silver River and turned off on the only exit. The sign that announced the entrance to the town said the population was a thousand people.

Main Street was maybe four blocks long featuring a hardware store that also sold bait for fishing and a drugstore that advertised a counter where you could order a meal.

"Not a lot to do around here," Hope remarked.

Road signs indicated that there was a park on the edge of town, and he could see what must be the school at the end of the street. "We'll just stay here for a bit, then go somewhere else. I think the smart thing to do is to not stay in one place too long."

The last thing he wanted was to lead anyone

straight to the cabin or to his friend's house. The more they stopped and started, the more likely they'd be able to shake someone tailing them. In a town this size, the assassin on the motorcycle wasn't likely to show himself. He had to assume that Zimmerman was still after them as well.

"I want to call Lawrence to make sure he's okay. I'm worried that doing this will put him in danger," she said.

"The movers won't show up until tomorrow." Andrew found a shady place to park that was adjacent to the post office, which was next to a bank. "I need to stretch my legs if you want to make the phone call." He handed her the phone. "I won't go far."

She took it from him and began dialing. He pushed open his door and stepped out onto the sidewalk. A group of four kids came up the sidewalk on bicycles. They whizzed past him.

When he strolled past the hardware store, he noticed that it had a camping and outdoor section. Some water bottles by the checkout counter caught his attention as well.

He moved only a short distance before turning around and looking back toward the car, where Hope sat in the passenger seat.

Through the window, he watched her take the phone away from her face and shake her head. Apparently, she hadn't been able to reach Lawrence.

He walked toward her side of the car and she rolled down the window.

"He didn't answer. I sent a text as well. Andrew, I'm worried. What if they got to him?"

He touched her arm where it rested on the windowsill. More than anything, he wanted to relieve her distress. Despite his resistance, he felt a connection to her. And yet, opening his heart completely to her was risky because what if, despite his efforts to keep her safe, he still lost her to the threat that hung over her life? He couldn't survive that kind of tragedy again. He tried to sound reassuring. "We don't know anything for sure. He could just be away from his phone. We'll try again in a bit. Like I said, if someone was watching his place, they wouldn't be alarmed until the movers showed up."

"Thank you, Andrew, you're probably right." Her demeanor was calmer.

He was glad his words could have that effect on her. "Let's go get some basic supplies in that hardware store and then we can get moving." The distraction would do them both some good.

Once inside, Andrew bought some energy bars, dehydrated food and the water bottles along with a backpack to put them in.

After they left Silver River, the landscape turned to fields of cows and farmland. The next town was fifty miles away.

Traffic was light, which made Andrew take notice of the white truck that came up behind them and didn't pass even when he slowed down.

Hope glanced nervously behind her. "The windows are tinted. I can't see the driver."

Andrew sped up and the truck remained close. His heart pounded as he gripped the wheel.

He saw the motorcycle only for a second in the side-view mirror before the first shot was fired. The bullet pinged the exterior of his car.

"He's shooting at us!" she cried.

"It's okay. Hang on." His adrenaline surged as he focused on the road up ahead.

The motorcycle had sped ahead of them but then suddenly slowed down. There were no other cars on this stretch of road.

Andrew slowed down, too, not wanting to give the motorcycle assassin another chance to shoot at them.

The white truck bumped the back of Andrew's car and he veered off the road to avoid another encounter with the man on the motorcycle. They rumbled through a field until they came to a fence.

He followed the fence to where it ended. The white truck was still coming toward them. There was a dirt road where the fence ended. "Guess we're going this way." While he had no idea where it led to, he had no choice but to take it.

The motorcycle was headed toward them as well. Hope swiveled in her seat. "He's getting closer."

He saw only open land up ahead and a sign indicating there was a fishing access not far away. "I hope this doesn't dead end. We'll be caught."

His pulse skyrocketing, he pressed the accelerator to the floor and drove as fast as he could. The white truck fell out of view, but the motorcycle still tailed them.

Andrew tried to keep the panic at bay. But it was difficult not to give in to it because he couldn't go back the way they came. The truck was probably waiting for him to return. He prayed this road would lead them back to the highway.

The fishing access was a giant reservoir without much greenery around it. Two boats were in the middle of the water, so far away they appeared to be miniatures.

Hope still held his phone. "Do you suppose a map of this place would come up on GPS?"

"It's worth a shot," he answered.

The road ended at the fishing access. The motorcycle was still behind them. Andrew kept driving as the terrain became rougher. The motorcyclist slowed as he avoided rocks and shrubs.

Hope huffed a frustrated breath as she stared at the phone. "All it shows is the lake. No roads."

The engine made a groaning and clanking noise

as Andrew climbed a rocky hill. "We have to keep going. We can't go back the way we came."

He inched forward until the shrubs turned into small trees.

But then he was forced to gun the engine as branches got caught in the tires and swished against the body of the car.

"We can't go any further in the car," he muttered. It seemed foolhardy to leave the car, but what option did they have?

He assessed how far they had gone on this road. Two, maybe three miles was his best guess.

Hope peered through the rearview mirror. "What now?"

As Andrew pressed the gas, the motor groaned and the wheels ground to a halt. He turned to look at her. "We have to make it back to the road on foot. Catch a ride." He grabbed the backpack of supplies he'd bought.

She met his gaze and nodded. They both got out of the car and ran toward the cover of the trees in the approximate direction the road had been.

As they ran, he thought he heard the faint sound of a motorcycle in the distance.

Hope's feet pounded the ground. She prayed they were headed in the right direction. It would be easy enough to get turned around and lost once they left the main road. And now all she saw in front of her was trees.

She tuned her ears to her surroundings, hoping to catch the distant sound of cars whooshing by on the highway, but only the noise of the forest reached her ears. From time to time, she thought she heard the hum of a motorcycle engine.

They jogged until they were out of breath and still all they encountered was more evergreens and brush.

Finally, the two of them slowed to a brisk walk as the sun grew low on the horizon. She feared they were headed deeper into wilderness.

"I don't hear the motorcycle anymore," she said.

There was a sort of trail through the trees that a skilled biker might be able to follow, but maybe he had given up or decided it would be more efficient to pursue them on foot.

"I haven't heard it for a while, either." Andrew's breathing had become more even once they weren't running. He walked a little faster.

After about twenty minutes, both of them broke into a jog again. They hurried as the sky grew grayer, signaling the arrival of evening. After a while, the two of them stopped and rested, each having a drink from their water bottles. She relished the coolness of the liquid going down her throat. "How much longer do we keep going in this direction?"

"I know, it seems like we should have come to the road by now," he said. "The first gut instinct is usually the right one. So I say we keep going this way. We might just be moving at a diagonal toward the highway so it's taking longer."

Turning in a different direction meant that risked encountering the motorcycle assassin.

She nodded and prepared to keep moving. More than once, she'd glanced over her shoulder and had not seen or heard any sign of the motorcyclist. That didn't mean they were safe.

The trees thinned, and she became hopeful that they would see some sign of civilization soon.

In an instant, she heard the roar of a motorcycle. A gun was fired close to her head, breaking the tree branch above her.

"Watch out!" Andrew wrapped his arm around her and hurried her toward a cluster of evergreens as another shot was fired.

The terrain was rough enough that the motorcyclist had to stop and steady himself on the bike before taking another shot at them.

They both burst into a sprint. The ground was bumpy and populated with sagebrush and rocks. She knew that a handgun was only accurate at close range. All they had to do was keep their distance from the motorcycle assassin.

As they ran, she started to notice trash—an old shoe, a bag, a soda can. They must be getting closer to where people were.

The motorcycle closed in on them as they came to a river. They stood on the bank staring at the rushing water. Through the trees and the dimming light, it looked like there was some kind of structure in the distance. And she thought she heard the sound of vehicles on a road, or was her mind playing tricks on her?

"We got no choice here," Andrew said. He plunged into the river.

It was quite wide, but it was impossible to tell how deep it was.

Still, she followed him. Within seconds, the water was up to her waist and then she was slicing her arms through it and being carried downriver.

She caught a glimpse of the motorcyclist on the opposite shore moving down the bank, probably looking for a shallow place to cross or even a bridge.

She worked her way toward the shore even though the current was strong. She reached out for a wedged log, pulling her head above water and catching her breath. Panic swept through her. She couldn't see Andrew anywhere.

A shot was fired close to her. She dived underwater and kept swimming. After she drifted downriver a ways, she bobbed to the surface to calculate how far she was from the bank and get a breath. When she glanced at the distant shore, she didn't see anyone. The current was so strong that fighting it was pointless. She only hoped it would carry her to the other side of the river quickly. She prayed Andrew would be okay as well.

Her feet touched rocks and she trudged the remaining distance to the far shore. When she looked around, she didn't see either man or the motorcycle.

She'd drifted some distance from where she thought she'd seen a structure through the trees. Soaking wet, Hope pulled herself up on the bank and started to walk upriver. After a few minutes of not seeing either man, she called out Andrew's name but not loudly. She trudged ahead as the water dripped off her, and she scanned the river fearing she would see his body floating.

That possibility hit her like a blow to her stomach. She took in a jagged breath and tried to compose herself.

Hearing what had to be the far-away mechanical clang of cars gave her the incentive to break into a run. She came to the back of a brick structure, the square building she'd noticed earlier. As she hurried toward it, picnic tables and a lawn with brown patches came into view as well. She was on the backside of a rest stop.

Noise behind her caused her to whirl around. Someone was breaking through the trees and coming toward her.

Her heart pounded as she looked for a place to hide.

FIFTEEN

Andrew's heart burst with gratitude when he saw Hope trying to slip behind a tree. He ran toward her and gathered her into his arms.

"You made it," he said.

"Oh, Andrew, I was worried about you, too," she gushed while he held her against him. "I'm so glad you're okay."

They pulled free of the embrace and hurried toward the brick structure, which became more defined as they got closer.

From what he could see of the parking lot, it was in need of repair. The picnic table as well had broken boards on it. This had been a rest stop but was no longer in use.

Off in the distance, a car went by on the road. Maybe someone would stop to stretch their legs, but it wasn't likely.

Andrew took the lead as he moved toward the side of the building preparing to step to the front.

His eyes landed on the motorcycle with a helmet hung on the handlebars.

He grabbed her and pulled her against the wall.

"He's there," Andrew whispered. "At least his motorcycle is. He must be hiding somewhere."

The hope that he had had that they might be able to get a ride from someone who pulled in here was dashed. The motorcycle assassin must have found a bridge and come across the river.

They stood for a long moment, their backs pressed against the cool brick, both of them soaking wet and exhausted.

"My guess is he is waiting for us to step out into that front parking lot and head toward the road." Andrew let out a breath. "He must be watching for us. I wish I knew where he was hiding."

"We won't know until he shoots at us and then it might be too late." Hope spoke in a whisper as well.

Both of them were aware that the gunman might be very close.

Andrew pushed off the wall and pointed in the direction they needed to go. First to the picnic table and then to a bin that held trash cans. "Stay low. Move fast."

Thankfully, they made it to the picnic table without a shot being fired. Andrew studied the shadows around the trees looking for anything that might be human. Another car whizzed by on the road.

Flagging someone down would be close to impossible. The cars were going too fast.

Hope pressed close to Andrew. He turned and nodded, tilting his head toward the trash can receptacle. They were only feet away from it when a shot was fired. Andrew pulled his gun and fired back.

They had to circle around to the side of the receptacle to avoid the next shot. The guy was in the bushes on the opposite side from where his motorcycle was parked.

This was their chance to get away.

"To the motorcycle," Andrew hissed.

They burst out running as two more shots were fired. The assassin was advancing at a rapid pace but standing still to take the shots.

Andrew reached the bike. The key was still in the ignition. He turned it and the motorcycle roared to life. He got on and prepared to push the kickstand up.

The man was running toward them but not shooting. Had he run out of bullets? Hope swung her leg over the back of the bike just as the man grabbed Andrew and yanked him off it. She saw then that he was the same man who had pursued them in Whitetail, blond hair, square jaw and big eyes.

Hope jumped off before the motorcycle clattered to the pavement. The man landed several blows to Andrew's face, causing him to stumble backward.

Hope picked up the helmet from the ground. She threw it at the assailant, hitting him in the head.

The move allowed Andrew to get the upper hand. He swung a fist at the man's head and then his stomach. The assailant bent over. Andrew landed two kicks to the back of his knees so the man fell to the ground. Andrew hit him on his back.

He stared at the bike, knowing there was not time to get it up and running before the assailant came after them again. Instead, he reached over and pulled the key out.

"Give me that." The man rose to his feet and lunged toward Andrew, taking him to the gravel.

Hope pummeled him with the helmet again, causing him to back off. Andrew got to his feet, and they both took off running with the gunman close behind them.

They ran toward the road. When a car went by, they waved frantically, but it didn't stop. They crossed the road into the forest. The man caught up to them and tackled Hope just as Andrew lunged toward where the assassin lay on Hope's back. The assailant drew a knife from a sheaf.

Andrew grabbed the man's wrist when he raised the knife to plunge it into Hope's back. He put his free hand on the man's chest and punched upward, praying Hope would get out from the under the weight of his body.

The rage in the attacker's eyes was frightening as he yanked Andrew's hand away from his chest. But Andrew managed to keep the hand that held the knife inert and above the man's head. He drove his free hand in an upward punch underneath the man's chin, sending him backward.

Andrew stepped forward preparing to get the knife where it had fallen on the ground. There was no time to pull his gun. The man turned sideways and grabbed the knife. He jumped to his feet and lunged at Andrew, who stepped out of the way.

Hope had risen from the ground. While the man's focus was on Andrew, she'd moved behind him and slammed a rock into his head.

The man crumpled to the ground and lay still.

"We have time to get back to the motorcycle. I still have the key." He took off running before he finished his sentence.

Hope sprinted beside him. They had to stop at the road to let a car zoom by. The driver was going so fast he barely looked in their direction.

They got to the motorcycle. "Lift from the handlebars," he told her. "I'll push on the frame."

They managed to get the bike a few inches

off the ground. He turned so his back was to the bike, so he could use the full strength of his legs like a lever. Once the bike was upright, he got on and turned the key in the lock. The bike sputtered and roared to life, but the headlight did not come on. The bulb must have gotten broken in the fall.

Hope got on behind him.

Though the bike had started, he noticed when he turned that something felt awkward. The handlebars may have been bent. The bike wobbled as he putted toward the road. There was vibration in the handlebars.

The assassin had risen to his feet and was headed in their direction. He must be in contact with the man who had been in the white truck.

Once he was out on the highway, Andrew wasn't able to go any faster than thirty miles an hour without the wobble becoming pronounced.

Until he saw a highway designation sign indicating what town lay ahead, he wasn't even sure where they were.

With the dusk of evening falling, he prayed the bike would hold up until they could get to relative safety. But he knew it wouldn't last long. The man on the motorcycle would probably alert the man in the truck, whom Andrew suspected was Jason Zimmerman.

They were far from free and clear from being attacked again.

* * *

As the vibration in the bike seemed to intensify, Hope held on to Andrew, wrapping her hands around his waist and leaning close. She had yet to see a sign that might indicate what road they were on or if any towns were close by.

Not only did the condition of the bike cause them to go slow, but without a headlight, Andrew probably could only see a short stretch of road in front of him. Also, there was a danger that if they did encounter a car, they might be hit because they were not visible.

When a sign finally came up indicating that the next town was seven miles away, she breathed a sigh of relief. She pressed her cheek against Andrew's back and held on to him, grateful for the safety she felt when she was close to him.

Gradually the lights of Polaris, Wyoming, came into view. The welcome sign informed her that thirteen hundred people lived here. As they puttered toward the main street of town, it looked like many of the businesses had already closed for the day.

Andrew parked in front of a café that was still open and next to the flashing neon sign advertising a bar.

She got off the bike.

A man and a woman headed toward the café did a double take when they saw Hope. She'd been running through forest, shot at and dunked in a river.

Andrew stared down at his clothes as well. "I bet we look like a couple of drowned rats."

"Or like we just blew into town," she deadpanned.

They both laughed. The moment of levity between them was a welcome reprieve.

"I'm starving, but I don't think we should go to the restaurant looking like this," he said.

She glanced up the street. The windows of the ranch supply place, which looked like it also sold clothes, were dark.

"Looks like most places shut down at night," she said.

"Guess we don't have a lot of options. Let's eat. Once I figure out where we ended up in relationship to where we need to be, I'll call my friend Dean. He might be a long drive away, but I don't think we will get very far on that motorcycle."

The mention of his friend reminded her that she still had not gotten hold of Lawrence.

Hope self-consciously smoothed over the soiled shirtfront and ran her hands through her hair. The shirt Julie had loaned her had been big in the first place. She shrugged. "What I wouldn't give for a hot shower and a hairbrush…"

"You look fine." He offered her a smile that made her heart flutter.

They entered the café, which was about two-thirds full.

The waitress's gaze rested on them for an uncomfortable moment before she spoke up. "Take a seat anywhere you want."

They found a booth toward the front of the café and settled in. The waitress placed water and menus in front of them. "The special is up on the board. Big plate of spaghetti with side salad and garlic toast."

Hope took a gulp of her water, which seemed to splash in her stomach. "I think I'm just going to get the special. I imagine they bring that out pretty fast."

Once the waitress returned, they ordered. The spaghetti showed up within minutes. At first, they both ate without talking while conversations from other diners buzzed around them.

The meal never tasted so good.

Andrew sopped up the last bit of spaghetti sauce with his bread. "My wife used to make spaghetti like this."

There was just a tinge of emotion in Andrew's voice. She knew it had taken courage for him to pull back the curtain on his personal pain. "You must miss her a great deal."

He nodded soberly. "But you understand about losing someone you love."

She was honored that he felt comfortable

enough to share with her. "Yes, it leaves a big hole inside of a person."

They stared at each other across the table for a long moment. Two people thrown together by violent circumstances. Both having losses that formed a bond between them.

Andrew looked away. He wiped his mouth and put down his napkin. "Why don't we find a quiet place to make some phone calls. See if we can get some help."

Hope rose to her feet but sat back down as shock waves surged through her when she glanced out the window.

Andrew leaned toward her. "What is it?"

"There's a white truck right outside that looks like the one that came after us earlier today." Hope sank deeper into her seat. Her ears buzzed from the intensity of the fear that enveloped her.

"Maybe it just looks like the one that followed us." He lifted his head and glanced out the window. His expression changed as his jaw grew tight. "Same dented front fender." Andrew's voice came out in a harsh whisper. "We have to get out of here."

SIXTEEN

Andrew surveyed the room, then looked at the door, half expecting to see Zimmerman entering the café. It wouldn't be hard to figure out where they were. The motorcycle was outside and not much was open at this hour.

"Come with me through the kitchen," he said. "Keep your back to the front windows."

After throwing down some money for the meal, both of them rose and headed toward the counter, where several men sat eating dinner. As they slipped through the kitchen doors, Andrew heard the waitress say. "Hey, you can't go in there."

The kitchen had only two staff, a man at the grill and a teenage boy loading the dishwasher.

"How do we get outside?" Andrew said.

The cook pointed toward the other end of the kitchen. The door must be down a hallway.

The waitress came into the kitchen. "What are you two doing? You can't be back here."

"We're just leaving." Andrew took Hope's hand and led her toward where the back door was supposed to be.

They moved down a short hallway. Andrew opened the door, and they stepped out into a dark alley where there was a dumpster. No light from the street reached the area.

They crouched by the trash receptacle. "Zimmerman wasn't in the cab of that truck. My guess is he's prowling around looking for us. He must have picked up his junior assassin on the motorcycle to be able to find us so quickly."

"We need to find a place to hide and call your friend," Hope said.

They had taken only two steps when the back door swung open. They were face-to-face with the motorcycle assassin.

Both of them burst forth running out toward the lighted side street. They headed toward Main Street, where they were more likely to encounter people. The hit man was right behind them.

When they got to Main Street, Jason was standing on the sidewalk half a block from the café. The blond man came around the block.

The two men closed in on them from either side just as a group of people spilled out of the bar next to the café. The motorcycle assassin turned to the side and leaned against the building. Zimmerman stopped approaching as well.

As the group of about eight people headed up the street, Andrew and Hope fell in on the side of them. Zimmerman edged toward them but kept his distance.

Once they were past the motorcycle assassin, Andrew said, "Excuse me," and pushed through the group of people while he held Hope's hand.

Using the crowd and the darkness as a shield and knowing that the motorcycle assassin wouldn't see them for a few seconds, he took off at a jog, pulling Hope with him. He slipped in behind a parked truck, lifting his head just above the truck bed.

The body language of both men told him neither had seen where he and Hope had hidden. Still glancing around, Zimmerman stomped up the street, headed toward where they were crouching behind the truck bed. The other man disappeared from view searching elsewhere.

Andrew led Hope toward the back bumper of the truck just as Jason walked by on the sidewalk.

They hurried across the street, where all the buildings were dark, taking refuge in between cars and hiding in the shadows.

Andrew looked back in the direction Jason had come. They sprinted in the opposite direction, at first using the cars as cover and then, when they were a few blocks away, staying in the darkness created by the eaves on the building. Up ahead, he saw a large building. The sign in front indicated it was the high school. What caught his eye was that one of the loading docks had a garage door that was open with light spilling out of it.

They could hide there and make the call to his friend.

They walked casually across the lawn toward the building. When they got to the loading dock, a truck was there but no one was around. They slipped inside what appeared to be the area where the cafeteria food and supplies were delivered, judging from the labels on the boxes.

They ran through an unlit cafeteria, up a hallway and into the library, which was also dark. Andrew and Hope settled in behind a bookshelf in the back of the room. He pulled out his phone.

One of the books on the oversize-books shelf caught Hope's eye, and she picked it up. "It has maps of Wyoming. I'm going to figure out where Polaris is in relationship to Cheyenne. That's where your friend lives, right?"

There was something endearing about Hope's need for information and ability to gather it. He had to admit that he found his heart opening up to her.

Andrew pulled his phone out. "I'll just call Dean. When I tell him where we are, he'll probably know how far off track we got."

He pressed in the number. It rang three times and went to voice mail.

Both Hope and Andrew jerked when they heard a loud thump. It sounded like it had come from the library entrance. He turned his phone off while the voice mail message was still playing and put it in his pocket.

Hope had stopped turning the pages of the book where it lay on her legs.

Footsteps, slow and far apart, reached his ears. Someone was in the library. It had to be one of the assassins.

His heart pounded as the footsteps grew louder. He saw a flash of light. They'd be spotted if the assailant shined the light in this corner. Both of them scrambled to the side of the bookshelf that faced the wall, pressing their back against the hard wood of the shelf.

Hope had left the book on the floor.

A cone of light traveled across the carpet off to Andrew's side. He tensed and held his breath as the light remained there close to where Hope had left the book.

If they moved, they risked making noise and being found. If the man chose to step toward where they were hiding, they would be spotted.

Both of them remained still as the seconds ticked by.

The light receded from the area where they

were, but the thump of footsteps seeming to echo around them continued. Andrew could hear his own intake of breath as Hope's shoulder pressed against his.

Even after the footsteps faded as the assassin moved from the muffled carpet of the library to the vinyl of the hallway, they stayed still.

Hope looked at him with a question in her eyes. *Is it safe yet?*

Andrew shook his head. He wasn't sure. The man may have seen them run into the school and would keep looking until he found them. He probably wouldn't come back into the library unless he was walking by and heard noise. Andrew took his phone out and stared at it. Now was not a good time to call for help.

A few more minutes went by before Hope spoke in a whisper, "The soundproof booths in the band room."

"What?"

"You're worried about noise from making a call, right?" She pointed to the phone still in his hand.

He was amazed that she was able to know his train of thought from that single gesture. "Yes, exactly."

Outside, they heard footsteps in the hallway. They both fell silent until they faded. The fact that the assassin was returning meant he knew they were in the school. He would keep looking until he found them.

"On our way in, just outside the cafeteria there was a sign pointing to the band room. When that guy walked by just now, he was headed in the opposite direction," Hope explained.

He contemplated what to do. Staying here might not be a good idea. It couldn't be that big a school judging from the size of the town. The assassin might decide to search every area a second time. Yet, if they left the high school, they would be hard-pressed to find a place that was private enough to make a phone call, and Zimmerman was also probably patrolling the town looking for them.

"Let's hurry to the band room," Andrew finally said.

They rose to their feet, moved along the bookshelf and out to the hallway. Staying close to the wall, Hope led the way to the band room.

He glanced down the hallway, seeing nothing. He prayed there was plenty of rooms to search beyond the library.

The band room was small with only two soundproof booths. Once they were both inside, Andrew closed the door. They both crouched below the glass so they wouldn't be seen. If they were found in here, they would be easy targets in such a closed space with only one exit.

* * *

Hope felt the same sense of urgency she saw reflected in Andrew's expression as he pulled out his phone.

"I'm worried about Lawrence's safety, but you need to make your call first."

He pressed in the number. After a few seconds, he spoke. "Hey, Dean, glad I caught you. Long story but we're in a bit of a tangle here. I don't know how close you are to a little town called Polaris... Okay... We could meet you in an hour. I think the bar next to the café will be the only place that's open. We can rendezvous outside of there on the sidewalk... Text when you're in place. And, Dean, thank you."

He handed her the phone. She dialed her godfather's number, feeling a rising tension when he didn't pick up after three rings.

A groggy voice came on the line. "Yes, hello."

The anvil of worry that had wedged in her chest lifted. "Oh, Lawrence. It's so good to hear your voice! Listen, I don't have much time. Did everything go okay with the movers picking up Craig's stuff?"

"Yes, went real smoothly. A couple of guys came late in the day and loaded the boxes."

"And everything has been okay there with you? No strangers coming by or watching the house?"

"Not of late. I have to tell you that right after the trial, there was a car that went by on the road several times a day. Didn't belong to any of the neighbors. The road past my house turns into a dead end."

She gripped the phone tighter. So Lawrence may have been watched at some point. "Thank you for doing all this. For me and for Craig. Stay safe."

"Same to you, Hope," Lawrence said. "Please take care of yourself. Wish I could see you again. Give you a hug. But I want you to have a shot at some kind of a life."

Her throat tightened as tears warmed her eyes. "Love you."

Lawrence said, "Love you, too, kiddo."

She hung up and handed Andrew his phone.

Andrew leaned toward her. "You okay?"

"No, but I'll pull it together, 'cause I need to in order to stay alive, right?"

His hand covered hers. "You're a strong lady."

The warmth of his touch was like a soothing balm. And the intensity of his gaze made her lean toward him. She realized in that moment that she wanted him to kiss her. She drew back, clearing her throat. "I take it we need to find a place to hide for an hour."

"Yeah, wandering the streets is not a good idea. But almost nothing is open. Any ideas?"

"I saw a sign for the auditorium in the school. The catwalk would be a good hiding place. We wouldn't be visible."

"Okay, let's go," Andrew said.

He opened the door to the soundproof booth. His attention was drawn to the hallway, probably looking for the illumination the assassin's flashlight created.

Hope was right behind him as they moved quickly to the door and out into the dark hallway, walking by lockers and classrooms.

He hesitated.

She slipped in front of him, remembering where she'd seen the arrows that pointed toward the auditorium. As they worked their way up a ramp and around a corner, she could hear footsteps down another hallway. They were easy enough to detect in the silent building but hard to tell where they were because of the echo.

The assassin was still searching for them.

She hoped it was the right decision to stay hidden in the school. With Jason probably wandering the streets and beating every bush, there was no safe place to hide in this town.

SEVENTEEN

Andrew followed as Hope led the way into the auditorium. They moved quickly past the rows of seats and up on the stage. She seemed to know her way around a theater, leading him backstage to a set of narrow stairs. They came to a platform about four feet across that provided a place to sit with a view of the stage. Below it was a lighting grid that spanned most of the stage.

Hope drew her knees to her chest, so they weren't dangling. He did the same. They sat side by side staring at the empty stage.

The last time he'd heard the footsteps, they'd sounded far away. Maybe it was safe to talk in a whisper as long as he kept his ears tuned to noise beyond the stage.

"Were you a theater kid in high school or something?"

"Theater, speech and debate," she replied. "All the artsy stuff and I worked in the library. How about you?"

"I spent a lot of time on the football field and the track."

"Well, if we had been in the same high school, our paths probably never would have crossed," she said.

"Probably not." Funny that she was thinking about such a thing. He tried to picture Hope as a high school student. Probably just as positive and full of life as she was now.

"I wasn't big on going to the football games. Interesting how our lives have intersected now." She turned to look into his eyes. "I'm glad, though, that I got to know someone like you, Andrew."

He remembered a moment earlier when she had leaned toward him as if ready for a kiss, but then she had broken the connection. "This has certainly been an adventure. My job is never boring."

Her expression changed. The light seemed to go out of her eyes and her jaw tightened. "All part of the job, right?"

He realized he had said the wrong thing. "I didn't mean it that way. You have become more than a job to me." He wanted to grab her hand and hold it. But he realized that would send the wrong message. Even so, he couldn't deny he had an attraction to her. He'd felt it from the very beginning.

After she was given another new identity and place to live, it would probably put her at risk for him to continue to be her point of contact with the program. Even if he could see her, infrequent, clandestine visits were no way to have a relationship. "You're a very special person. After the sacrifices you've made, you deserve a normal life."

"I think I left normal behind when I chose to testify." A note of sadness permeated her words. "You and I are from different worlds. Just like we would have been in high school. I think you're a wonderful man, Andrew. Wish we could have met under different circumstances."

"Me, too. Stars colliding and all of that." He longed to tell her that in the five years since his wife had died, this was the first time he had even wanted to open his heart to the possibility of love, but even that might get her hopes up.

Silence fell around them. Andrew checked the time on his phone every ten minutes. Half an hour passed.

He heard footsteps and let out a sharp breath. The assassin was in the auditorium. A second later, light traveled across the stage. Thankfully, they were concealed from being seen from the front by a short curtain. Both of them had scooted to where the shadows hid them. The only way they could be spotted would be for the assailant to walk to the back of the stage and shine the light up.

They listened while the footsteps plodded toward the stage and then stepped onto it. The wooden floorboards of the stage creaked.

His heart squeezed tight. Hope's body stiffened next to him, indicating her level of fear. The assassin was right below them, though the platform kept them hidden.

The shooter moved to the other side of the stage. Andrew could hear a side curtain being pulled back, making a swishing noise.

The man searched a moment longer before going back down the stairs that led to the seats.

Andrew waited a few minutes after it sounded like the man had left the area before he pulled his phone out to check the time. "We have ten minutes to get to Main Street. Let's hope my friend wasn't delayed in any way."

Hope moved toward the stairs. "Hopefully, there is a back way out of the theater, so we don't have to go through the whole school again."

Once they were on the stage, they searched for a door that led outside but found none. The huge garage door was probably shut now by whoever had been doing deliveries. Most doors in a school were designed to open from the inside and then lock. All they needed to do was find the closest door and they would be out.

"I don't remember seeing any exit between here and the band room," Andrew said

"Me, either. There was one in the cafeteria."

"That's across the school." Too much of a chance of running into the assassin.

They moved through the carpeted auditorium and out into the locker-lined hallway. Andrew scanned the area hoping to see an exit sign.

Unfortunately, he had no idea which direction the assassin had gone. He stared down a hallway they hadn't explored. There was an arrow indicating the gym was that way. "Gyms usually have an exit to a playing field."

They went up the hall and around another turn. When they stepped into the gym, it was too dark to even see if there was a door. Shades had been pulled down on the windows, so not even moonlight provided illumination.

He pulled Hope back against the wall.

"I'm going to have to turn on the flashlight on my phone. We don't have time to let our eyes adjust to the darkness."

He stepped away from the open door, hoping the light wouldn't be seen in the hallway. Then to his dismay, he crashed into something metal. He heard the sound of balls rolling across the floor.

He turned on the flashlight for only a second, long enough to see that the exit door was on the other side of the gym. They ran toward it in the dark, slowed by the balls that had rolled across the gym floor.

Light flooded the room, and the assassin was

on top of them in seconds. Andrew felt the weight of a body on his back and then his stomach was pressed against the floor.

The attacker's flashlight rolled across the floor. Hope picked it up. He heard her retreating footsteps.

The guy grabbed the back of Andrew's head, preparing to smash it against the floor.

Right before his face impacted with the floor, he heard a thunking sound, and the weight of the other man shifted to one side.

Hope had found a bat and hit the man with it. *Brave woman.* She aimed the flashlight in the direction of the exit. Andrew crawled out from underneath of the now-unconscious man.

With Hope holding the flashlight, it was easy to navigate around the balls that were rolling across the floor. He pushed open the door, and they stepped out into the night.

They ran across a football field and rerouted toward Main Street. He hoped his friend was parked and waiting. He hadn't received a text yet.

If not, Andrew was pretty sure they'd have an encounter with Jason Zimmerman before they got out of town. If they got out of town.

Hope was out of breath by the time they reached Main Street. Not used to such a level of violence, she was still shaking from having used a baseball bat on a person. Though the café was now closed, the flashing neon and the noise spilling from open doors indicated that the bar was still open.

As they walked up the sidewalk, a tall, dark-haired man got out of a gray SUV and waved at them. That had to be Andrew's friend. She glanced up the street where another man slipped back into the shadows. That had to be Jason.

Andrew greeted his friend with a hardy slap on the back. "Boy, am I glad to see you."

"Same here."

Andrew opened the back door. "We should both sit in the back. It's safer."

She wondered if he had seen Jason as well.

Once Dean had started the car and shifted into Reverse, Andrew cupped his hand on his friend's shoulder. "Chances are we're going to be followed."

"I can handle that," Dean assured him. "I won't go directly back to my house."

"And for sure we don't want to lead them to your cabin when we go up there," Andrew said.

Once they were out on the highway, she rested her head against the back of the seat.

"Are you going to fill me in on what this little adventure is about?" His friend glanced in the rearview mirror.

Andrew sat up straighter and summarized all

that had happened and why they needed the use of the cabin. The tone of his voice changed when he spoke about the death of Bryson Whitman.

"Oh, man, that's too bad," Dean said. "He was never my direct supervisor when I was with the marshals, but I knew he was one of the good guys."

They drove for what seemed like hours. Hope dozed off. When she woke, they were rolling through a town.

Dean wound his way through several subdivisions in a serpentine pattern before coming to a stop in front of an older-looking home with a small front yard.

Hope sat up straighter, looking for signs that the truck had followed them. Jason would not be so obvious. If he had been able to track them here, he would have hung back in the white truck.

The house had no garage. Leaving his car parked on the street, Dean got out of the vehicle. Hope and Andrew stepped out onto the sidewalk as well. Dean unlocked the house door and they went inside. He switched on a light by the door.

A golden retriever emerged from a room and greeted his owner. "Hey, Jasper. Did you take care of the homestead for me?"

Dean walked with a limp. Must be from the injury that had caused early retirement.

The living room looked like it had been turned

into a fly-fishing workshop; rods and reels and fly-tying equipment were everywhere.

When Dean noticed her looking around, he quipped, "It's how you get to set up your living room when you're a single guy."

Hope couldn't help but smile.

Dean moved toward the kitchen and turned on a light. "Are you two hungry or thirsty?"

"I could use a drink of water." Hope followed Dean into the kitchen.

"Yeah, water sounds nice," Andrew concurred as he stepped into the bright kitchen.

Jasper entered the kitchen as well, lifting his head as though following the conversation.

Dean spoke while he pulled glasses from a cupboard and filled them up at the tap. "One of you can sleep on the couch and I got a camping cot I can set up in the living room. This place is not very big. I only got the one bedroom."

He handed the full glasses of water to Hope and Andrew.

"Thanks, man," Andrew said. "In the morning, we'll need to come up with a plan to make sure we're not followed to the cabin."

"I have some ideas," his friend said. "But it involves getting a second car." He petted Jasper's head and got rewarded with a tail wag. "Let's get you two settled, so you can at least have a good night's sleep."

Within a few minutes, the camping cot had been set up with blankets and a pillow. Andrew took the couch across the room.

Hope lay in the dark with her eyes open listening to the sound of Jasper breathing at the end of the bed. He seemed to have decided to be her personal bodyguard. At least if someone tried to enter the house, the dog would be on alert.

Though she was beyond exhausted, sleep did not come right away. The gentle snoring sounds coming from the couch indicated that Andrew had fallen asleep.

She knew that Jason would not give up easily. All the same, she found herself praying that everything would go smoothly tomorrow, and they would have answers as to what her brother had that the cartel wanted.

As long as he didn't see the contents of what was being brought to the cabin, Jason wouldn't have any way of knowing what their plan was. If he was going to attack them, it would be tonight. That thought did not help her sleep any better.

Any time the dog stirred, her eyes fluttered open. She heard Andrew get up several times in the night and walk the perimeter of the house, checking at each window.

Both of them knew it was too soon to think they were safe.

EIGHTEEN

Andrew sat at the kitchen table drinking coffee while Dean stood at the stove breaking eggs into a bowl and beating them with a whisk. Jasper positioned himself between the stove and table, watching for any crumb that might fall to the floor. He and Dean had been awake for about twenty minutes, talking over the best way to get to the cabin once they got word the boxes had been delivered.

Hope came in from the living room. The bags under her eyes meant she hadn't slept well, either.

"Just in time for breakfast," Dean said brightly.

Andrew rose and poured her a cup of coffee while she sat down.

She muttered a thank-you.

Jasper left his post to get a head pat from her.

The eggs made a sizzling noise when Dean poured them along with some vegetables he'd cut up into the cast-iron pan.

Andrew took another sip of his coffee. "Dean

has a plan for us to get up to the cabin without being detected."

"You think we were followed here?"

"Based on Zimmerman's past behavior, I think it's safer to assume that than to believe that we shook him," Andrew told her. "His friend on the motorcycle might have hitched a ride, too."

Even though they had left him unconscious, he might have recovered.

Hope rubbed her eyes. "You're probably right. But wasn't last night the perfect chance to come after me?"

Andrew shrugged. "Maybe he's watching and waiting, trying to figure out what we're up to, which is even more reason why he can't know why we're going to that cabin."

Dean served up the eggs and set a plate in front of Hope and Andrew. Toast, butter and jam were already on the table. Then he sat down with his own plate. "Actually, I have two plans. The first is pretty straightforward. I take you up there and stand guard. Andrew is not crazy about that one—"

"The second plan involves borrowing another car," Andrew interjected.

Hope seemed to have perked up after a few sips of coffee. She took a bite of eggs and slathered some butter on her toast. "We have to wait to hear from the movers that the stuff was even delivered first, right?"

Andrew nodded and pointed to his phone. "They're supposed to text me when they deliver the stuff. Hopefully, in a few hours."

"I went up there and unlocked the cabin. No big deal in the short term," Dean said. "Mice and squirrels are the bigger culprits more than anything."

"What's the second plan?" she asked.

"We make arrangements to have a car parked with the keys in it at a store that has a front and back entrance. There are several places in town that will work. We all three go inside. You guys slip out the back and get in the car. The tail will be focused on watching my car."

"Dean would just need to find a friend willing to loan us a car." Andrew watched as a look of wariness came over Hope's face again.

She took a nibble of toast. "That sounds really involved."

"I'll make some calls. We'll figure it out," Dean promised.

They finished their breakfast, then their host gathered up the plates. "I'm going to take a shower. There is a powder room for you to freshen up in or you can use the shower after I'm done." He excused himself.

Hope rose to her feet and stepped toward the kitchen door when Jasper stood and whimpered. "Looks like the backyard is fenced."

She opened the door and followed Jasper out. Andrew got up as well. The yard had a high fence with several raised beds with vegetables growing in them. They took a seat on a bench in the corner.

Jasper set a toy at Hope's feet, and she tossed it for him. A look of genuine pleasure came across her face as she played with the dog.

Andrew sat back on the bench and watched the interaction. "You didn't sleep much last night, did you?"

"Nope. But I could say the same about you even though you fell asleep right away." She tossed the toy and the dog leaped for it. "Don't you think if he was able to follow us, he would have attacked us by now?"

"I know that you're tired of all of this, but we can't let our guard down just because he hasn't made an appearance in eight hours," Andrew reminded her.

She shook her head and let out a heavy breath. "I just want it to be over."

"I know you do. So do I. But we have to stay vigilant. I saw him on the street back in the shadows as Dean pulled out back in Polaris."

"I know, I did, too," she admitted.

"Remember, Zimmerman and his buddy are hired help. If we don't figure out who leaked your new identity info, we won't be able to relocate you with a reasonable assurance of safety."

"I'm just worried that we're leading Jason to the very thing he was looking for. The only reason to keep me alive for a few extra seconds was to get an answer to that question about my brother's things."

"But he would have found some other way to figure it out if you didn't tell them."

"True." She sighed. "That must be why Lawrence's place was being watched. I'm sure they figured out who the other important people in my old life were. They just didn't have the manpower to watch everyone all the time."

He turned to face her. "Hope, if you want any kind of a life, we've got to go through with this plan."

"What if I just decided to live in one of those little towns we drove through, forget thinking that I need WITSEC's help," she murmured.

He sensed that her frustration and fear had made her say something so radical. "You'd need ID and money to get set up. It's not as easy to hide as you think it might be."

Tears rimmed her eyes. "Andrew, I'm worn out. It's like being punished for having done the right thing and put a bad man in jail."

Andrew's heart squeezed tight. She had been so strong for so long. He gathered her into his arms. "It's okay. A lesser person would have fallen apart way sooner." He held her for a long moment, relishing how good it felt to comfort her, but wishing he could take the heartache away.

"Thank you, Andrew," she whispered. "For staying with me through all this."

He pulled back and held her face in his hands so he could look into her brown eyes. "We'll get through this. And you'll have a new life in a safe place. If you can just hang on for a little while longer."

She nodded, holding his gaze. "I'll do my best."

He leaned in, gently brushing his lips against hers. When he pulled back, the trust he saw in her eyes made him kiss her again.

Long moments later, he stared down at her beautiful face. He saw now that he could care about a woman again, but he also knew the situation was hopeless. Once this was all over, Hope would be whisked away with a new name to a different place.

Jasper let out a yip. Hope turned her attention back to the dog, breaking the moment of connection between them.

After Dean finished his shower, he was able to get a friend to agree to leave a car at the local ranch supply place. Andrew received the text that the boxes had been delivered.

They drove across town and walked into the supply shop.

After giving his friend a nod, they worked

their way toward the back. The plan was that Dean would wait in the store until they had had ample time to find the car and get out of the lot. If the front of the lot was being watched, once Dean came out by himself, it would be clear to the assassins what they had done.

Andrew pushed open the back door, and they stepped into the lot where the employees probably parked. It took only a few minutes to spot the car that his pal had described. After checking for the keys under the passenger floor mat, Andrew sat behind the wheel.

Hope got into the passenger seat.

He took a street that would not lead them past the front lot of the store. Then he handed Hope his phone and recited the location of the cabin for her so she could punch it into GPS.

The drive took them out of town and up a winding country road. Though there had been cars behind them all through town and out onto the highway, they were alone once they were close to the cabin.

Dean's hunting cabin, tucked back in the trees, came into view. He parked in the dirt driveway. "Let's hope we find what we are looking for," Andrew said.

Hope stared at the front door of the cabin, praying it would become clear why something her brother had was of value to the cartel. She unbuckled her seat belt and followed Andrew inside. Eight large boxes sat just inside the door of the one-room cabin. No labels had been put on any of them.

"I have no idea what we're even looking for." She stepped toward a box and pulled the tape off that kept it sealed. The sight of her brother's coats and neatly folded clothes made her chest feel like it was in a vise.

Andrew must have sensed her emotional shift. He stepped toward her and rubbed her back. "This might bring up ugly memories. Stop and take a break when you need to."

His sensitivity to how the situation made her feel reminded her of the kiss they'd shared. How being in his arms felt like coming home to a warm house with a fireplace.

Though she was sure the pictures in her head from the night of the shooting would not be kept at bay, her immediate reaction was to feel the depth of Craig's loss. She really had not even been given time to mourn his passing. "Mostly, it makes me think about how much I loved my brother."

She pulled the coat out and checked the pockets, placing the keys she found on a shelf by the door. Though one of them looked like a house key, maybe one of the other keys was important.

Andrew scooted a box over to the couch and sat down to pull things out. She watched as he placed an acoustic guitar to one side after examining the body and angling it side to side to see if there was anything inside. Maybe her brother had hidden drugs somewhere.

She worked through the box containing mostly clothes and then opened another one that was filled with kitchen items. Hope looked in each canister she pulled out, wondering if Craig had stashed something important inside. She pulled the tape off the flour container, which felt heavy for the amount of flour that was in it. She shook it.

"Canisters are a very common hiding place," Andrew noted.

Glad they were both on the same wavelength, she stuck her hand in the can of flour. She felt something hard. Her breath caught when she pulled out a small-caliber gun.

"Was he in the habit of keeping a gun for protection?"

"Not that I know of. This must have been a recent purchase." Holding the gun by the handle, she set it on the shelf by the keys.

"If he registered it, we would be able to trace when he purchased it," Andrew said.

They worked through several more boxes, not finding anything else of interest. It wasn't until they found two boxes that had been taken from

Craig's office that they slowed down. She set the laptop and printer to one side. Craig had binders filled with columns of numbers as well as envelopes that had receipts that clients must have given him. Some had the name of the person or business written on it.

Hope came across a box that stored thumb drives labeled only with the year and some with no label at all.

"What do you suppose this means?" Andrew handed her a sheet of legal-sized paper he'd pulled from an envelope.

She stared at it for a long moment. "It's Craig's handwriting." The drawing had a series of circles with names of people and businesses written in them along with arrows to other names and businesses.

Andrew held up a pile of papers. "These receipts were in the same envelope." He handed them to her.

She filed through the receipts. There were too many to check all of them but some of the names on the receipts matched names written on the piece of paper. Apparently, Craig was trying to make some sort of connection between the businesses and the way money was being moved around.

Another box contained more office materials and an odd assortment of items, some with business logos on them. Everything from notepads, baseball hats to water bottles.

Andrew held up several of the items that referenced a sports drink. "I feel like I have seen this logo somewhere else."

She picked up a bandanna with a logo for a dog treat on it. "These are promotional things his clients give him. And I recognize some of the names from that paper and the ledgers."

He showed her the baseball cap with the sports drink logo. "No, I mean I've seen this in another setting. I just can't place it."

"Maybe you saw the sports drink in a grocery store or a gym," she said.

He shook his head. "I don't think that's it..."

By the time they'd gone through all the boxes, the sky had turned gray outside.

Andrew rose to his feet and stretched. "We need to go before it gets dark. This car is borrowed. I'm sure they want it returned."

"But we're not done." She opened the last box and peered inside. It held framed photos and a painting as well as items that must have been in Craig's bathroom. Probably nothing in there, but if they were being thorough, they should look at the backs of the photos.

Andrew stacked several binders by the door. "Take the thumb drives and this laptop and that last box with you," he said. "We'll have to look at them later."

She stood back as a sadness overtook her. "What is going to happen to Craig's stuff?" These eight boxes represented her brother's life.

"Let's pack them back up. With Dean's help, we can figure out a permanent place to store them."

They worked quickly as the sun slipped even lower in the sky, loading up the items that seemed important. Afterward, Andrew locked the place up with the key that Dean had given him.

As he wound down the mountain toward the highway, Hope spoke her thoughts out loud. "I think the gun indicates my brother was afraid of something. Maybe he knew the Queen Bee Cartel was coming for him."

"But if it wasn't drug debt, what was it?"

She thought of the handwritten piece of paper where Craig appeared to be making financial connections between businesses and people. "I think it had something to do with his job as an accountant. We won't know until we look at the thumb drives. We can start with the most recent year and work our way back."

"It might take a forensic accountant to see what needs to be seen," he mused. "But it did seem like he was trying to connect the dots that the cartel was laundering money."

Andrew sped up once they were on the highway. She was looking forward to a shower and sleep. Even if it was on a camping cot, she had a feeling she wouldn't have trouble falling asleep tonight.

Once in town, they stopped at a fast-food place and got some tacos. When they parked in front of Dean's house, all the lights inside were off.

"Strange, it's not that late," Andrew said. "I'm a little concerned. Stay in the car and I'll go check it out."

Fear gripped her throat. "You think they came for your friend, when they couldn't find us?"

He pushed open the door. "I'm not sure but we're not taking any chances. Lock the doors. Wait until I come back."

Hope watched as Andrew stepped toward the door and opened it. He stepped inside. There was a flash like a burst of lightning.

She wheezed in a breath.

A gunshot?

She had to get out of this car, but she didn't want to lead Jason and the other man to the very thing they may have been looking for. Still, her gut told her Andrew needed her help.

Hope tried not to make a sound as she stepped out of the vehicle, locking the doors and crouching, watching the now-silent, dark house.

Where was Dean? Had Andrew been shot?

NINETEEN

From the floor where he lay, Andrew could hear soft footsteps. Some instinct for survival had made him plunge to the floor right before the shot was fired.

Though the assassin seemed to want the room to remain dark, Andrew eased toward a chair that would conceal him if the lights were turned on.

He assumed the shooter was trying to figure out if he had hit his target.

Playing along, Andrew made a moaning sound. If the guy thought he had been shot, maybe he would let his guard down. He feared, though, that the goal was to get him out of the way so the assassin could go after Hope. It had been a mistake to tell her to stay in the car. Hopefully, she had found a better hiding place.

From the backyard, he could hear Jasper barking. Andrew remained still, trying to assess what his next move should be. He still didn't know what had happened to Dean or if he was dealing with one or two assassins.

The moaning had made the man stop moving around the living room.

Andrew heard a noise coming from the kitchen that was almost concealed by Jasper's even more frantic barking. A door opening maybe? Had Hope come in the back way?

No. That would put her in danger.

The soft footsteps retreated to the kitchen.

Andrew rose to his feet and fumbled for a light switch. The living room flooded with light. He heard noises in the kitchen. A chair being knocked over. Another shot was fired.

As the breath compressed from his lungs, Andrew hurried toward the kitchen. No one was there, but the door had been flung open. Jasper greeted him, shaking and whining. He ran outside to the fence, where he saw the assassin, Zimmerman, disappear around a corner. He didn't see Hope anywhere.

He heard sirens in the distance. A neighbor must have heard the shots and called the police.

Andrew ran toward where the assassin had gone back down an alley but saw nothing. The arrival of the police might be enough to make the perp flee, but where was Hope?

He ran down the alley for several blocks as lights in other houses came on. After not finding her, he had no choice but to return to Dean's house. He entered through the back. The kitchen door was open and so was the front door, where the police lights flashed. Jasper paced the floor and made whining noises.

He caught a glimpse of Hope standing outside talking to the police and pointing. He ran to her and gathered her in his arms. She was out breath from running.

They both talked at the same time. "I was afraid you'd been shot."

The police officer standing close to Hope spoke up. "Were you involved in this incident?"

Andrew pulled free of the hug but kept his arm wrapped around her waist. "Yes, I'm with the US Marshals." Andrew showed his badge. "There is a man who took a shot at both of us."

"We're looking for him now," the officer told him.

"If I may go back in the house… My friend who lives here is missing," Andrew said. "I'm worried something may have happened to him."

The officer nodded. "This place is a crime scene at this point. I will go with you."

They entered the small house and both of them ran toward the bedroom. Dean had been tied up and gagged and left in the closet. But thankfully he seemed unharmed.

Andrew reached down to help his friend, pulling the duct tape off his mouth. "I am so sorry about this." He pulled out his pocketknife to cut the rope that bound his friend.

"Of course they staked out the house when they couldn't find you and Hope. They must have followed me from the ranch supply place thinking you would return here." Dean pulled the ropes off his hands and let them fall to the floor.

Once Dean was free, they all stepped back outside just as the forensics team showed up.

"These guys are probably going to be a while," Dean informed him. "I'm going to go around to the back of the house and get Jasper calmed down."

"We'll go with you," Andrew said.

When his friend entered the gate, Jasper gave all three of them an enthusiastic welcome. Dean spoke in a soothing tone to his dog. "A little too much excitement for both of us tonight, hey, buddy?"

Andrew and Hope took a seat on the bench while they watched Dean toss a toy for Jasper. Andrew's hand covered hers where it was resting on the bench.

They waited outside in the cool of the evening until the last forensic tech had left and an officer cleared them to enter the house.

Andrew turned toward the officer who stood

at the kitchen door. "Did they catch the guy who shot at us?"

The officer shook his head. "Not that I heard."

"He may come after us again," Andrew said.

"I'll see to it that an officer is parked outside." The policeman's footsteps echoed as he made his way to the front of the house.

Hope touched Andrew's arm. "We need to bring the stuff from the cabin in and put it in a secure place."

"You found something?" Dean was already headed up the back stairs with Jasper close behind him.

"We're not sure what it means...if anything," Hope confided.

"Hope, why don't you stay inside. Dean and I will get the stuff out of the car."

"I still have to get that car returned to my friend," Dean added. "I'll call him and have him come by."

Hope waited inside while Andrew and Dean retrieved the items from the car. The patrol car pulled up just as they were about to enter the house. The officer waved at them.

Andrew stared back up the dark street. Zimmerman might be out there watching them even now. Dean didn't have a garage. There was no way they could conceal that they had taken things from the car.

They entered the house.

Hope hurried across the room. "Here, let me take those." She lifted the binder and the box filled with thumb drives from his arms.

Andrew turned and made sure the door was locked and deadbolted. Still, he knew that if the assassin saw an opportunity to come after them again, a locked door wouldn't stop him.

Hope laid the binders on the kitchen table. Dean came in after her with the laptop and more binders.

"You know, I'm not tired," Hope murmured. "I think I'm going to start looking through these thumb drives."

Andrew stood in the doorway between the kitchen and living room. "I'm with you. Too much excitement to just lay down and fall asleep. I can help you."

"But there is only one laptop," Hope reminded him.

"I have a laptop you can borrow," Dean offered. "It's in the bedroom. I'll go get it."

Hope found the charger cord for her brother's laptop. "I'm thinking maybe there might be something on the hard drive that is important. We need to search everywhere."

"Was the laptop in plain sight the night your brother was shot?" he asked.

"I don't remember for sure. But Craig wasn't shot in his office. He was shot in the living room."

Andrew scrubbed a hand across his jaw. "It seems like if Lincoln Kramer knew what they needed was on the laptop, he would have grabbed it."

"I think my showing up interrupted that process. Craig was shot at night. He was in the habit of putting away his work at the end of the day. So now that I think about it, the laptop wouldn't have been out in the open." The memory of that night was etched on her brain because the lawyers had made her recall the details of what had happened. The killer had used a silencer on the gun. She had stepped into Craig's house through the open door and seen her brother on the living room floor.

A new memory surfaced that she hadn't been questioned about by the legal team. When she saw the killer, but he didn't see her before she slipped back outside, he had been looking in a drawer in the living room. He was searching for something.

Dean returned with the second laptop. "I for one am going to sleep like a log tonight after all the excitement. I'll see you two in the morning."

Andrew gave his friend a sideways hug. "Thanks for everything, man. And I am so glad you are okay." The two men clapped hands. "Way more excitement than you bargained for."

"Brings up the old days when I was with the marshals, so that's not a bad thing," Dean said. "I guess we're still on high alert here even with that cop outside. I'll get up in the night and check that all is well."

"I'll do the same," Andrew murmured.

Dean retreated to his bedroom.

Hope hit the power switch on the laptop and Craig's desktop came on the screen. Nothing on his desktop stood out. Her brother had some photos of Hope and Lawrence as well as one of him playing guitar. Her throat got tight when she clicked on one of them together on a hike. There were some invoices on the desktop as well.

She picked up the thumb drive with the most recent year on it. As she suspected, it was more ledgers and columns. Nothing that she could make sense of.

But giving up wasn't an option.

She grabbed one of the thumb drives that had no label on it. It was a series of photographs of people she didn't recognize other than Craig. They appeared to be at various celebrations or parties. One of the photos showed a cake with a banner above it that said: *Schedule Master LLC*. The name seemed familiar.

She looked across the table at Andrew, his face

only half-visible above the laptop. "Where's that piece of paper of Craig's diagram?"

Rising to his feet, Andrew retrieved the paper from one of the binders and passed it over to her. He remained standing, staring out the kitchen window. "You know, I think I'm going to do a quick patrol around the house and then make sure all the doors are locked." He glanced down at the golden retriever who lay at Hope's feet. "Jasper would probably appreciate one more potty run."

Hope tensed, a reminder that Jason might try to come back again.

Andrew opened the back door to let Jasper out. "I'll go talk to that officer as well. See if he noticed anything." He shut the door behind him.

Hope looked at the diagram. The business she saw in the photo was listed there. Andrew had come back in the house by the time she had matched two more businesses from the photos.

He opened the back door to let Jasper inside. The dog took up his position at Hope's feet while Andrew locked the door.

He sat back down. "Find anything?"

"Yes, my brother put together some photos of corporate events. Three of the businesses match the ones listed on Craig's diagram," Hope replied. "Plus, do you see that note at the bottom of the page on the diagram?

Andrew read out loud. "*Start-up Capital* with a question mark."

"What if the Queen Bee loaned drug money and charged interest for someone who wanted to start a business but couldn't get a loan from a bank? Wouldn't that be another way to make dirty money but a little cleaner?"

She filed through more photographs, stopping when she saw a face she recognized. Lincoln Kramer, the man who shot and Craig and she put in jail. Seeing his face sent a chill down her spine. "Guess what I found." She turned the screen so Andrew could see.

His eyes widened. "Wow. This means that legit business has a link to the Queen Bee Cartel."

TWENTY

Andrew's heart beat a little faster when he saw the photo of Lincoln Kramer. "You know what I think? I'm starting to believe your brother figured out who the Queen Bee was or at least was starting to see a connection between those companies and how money was being moved around."

"Craig put these photos together for a reason." Hope drew her attention back to the laptop. "If Lincoln Kramer made an appearance at the legit parties, maybe the Queen Bee did, too."

"I don't think she would be so careless as to pose," Andrew countered. "She'd probably avoid the camera so at best you might see her in the background."

"It's worth a shot." She scrolled through the pictures and then back again, going slower.

He sat down beside her and leaned toward the screen. In one of the posed photos, a woman bent her head and turned to the side as if she was camera shy. "There. I wonder if this woman is at any of the other functions."

Hope clicked through a fundraiser sponsored by the sports drink company. The same woman was in a photo leaning over the silent auction items. Clearly a candid shot, the photo barely showed her profile.

The woman had brown hair that half covered her face, and she dressed in neutral colors. "Sort of understated. Not what you would expect of someone who runs the biggest cartel in the western United States."

"I bet she dresses that way on purpose, so she fades into the background and isn't remembered," Hope speculated. "It is the same woman, though, at two different functions for different businesses."

"You might be right," Andrew said. "It would be good to have a name, but the important thing for us is figuring out who in WITSEC was feeding her information about you and lining up former hit men to come after you."

"Even with his addiction, Craig was a good accountant." Hope stared at everything on the table. "You know, if my brother was getting his drugs from the Queen Bee Cartel, they might have been throwing work his way, thinking his habit would give them the leverage in controlling him or even exchanging work for drugs.

Andrew rose to his feet and stretched. "Once he got sober, though, it would have been a whole different ball game."

"Exactly." Hope yawned. "I'm finally feeling like maybe I could fall asleep. Tomorrow we can figure out who this woman is. I suspect Craig may have figured it out, maybe he wrote it down somewhere. If we have a name to go on, it might indicate who in WITSEC was her source. If they ran in the same circles or are related."

Hope excused herself to freshen up in the powder room.

Andrew sat, feeling a strong sense of satisfaction. They probably had enough evidence to take to the DEA investigators, but Craig had probably made way more progress than anyone on figuring out who the Queen Bee was. An investigation into who was connected to those businesses might bring up a common name. But they didn't have time for that. They had to figure out who in WITSEC was feeding the Queen Bee information in order for Hope to reenter the program. Of course, that would mean he wouldn't see her again. The thought made his chest feel tight.

He heard Hope in the living room.

Sighing, he got up and went to the bathroom to splash water on his face. There was a tube of toothpaste in the medicine cabinet. He brushed his teeth with his finger.

Hope was underneath the blanket on the camping cot when he returned to the living room. Jasper lay at her feet.

"Looks like you've been adopted," he said.

She lifted her head and looked down at the dog. "He seems to like me."

"He feels a strong need to protect you." Andrew lifted his blanket and lay down on the couch. "I know the feeling."

"Won't be long now. I should be able to get a new identity that won't be compromised." A note of sadness came into her voice. "I'll be stepping into my new life."

Or was he just reading into what she had said because he knew he was going to miss being around her all the time? A bond had formed between them that would soon be severed. The memory of the kiss they'd shared still lingered.

With that thought on his mind, Andrew drifted off to sleep. He barely stirred when he heard Dean get up and check each of the windows in the house, reminding himself that he needed to do the same in a few hours.

He awoke from the fog of sleep.

While he waited for his eyes to adjust to the darkness, he rested on his elbows, listening. Jasper no longer lay at Hope's feet. He must have gone into Dean's bedroom when he'd gotten up.

He lifted the blanket and stood.

Andrew padded to the kitchen, got a drink of water and studied the area outside the yard for a long moment, searching the shadows for any kind of movement. With the police car parked in front of the house, an attack was most likely to come through the back door.

He stared at the thumb drives and laptops they'd laid out on the kitchen table. The name of Craig's accounting business was on the binders. If Zimmerman saw it, he would figure out what they had been up to. That they had gotten Craig's things. For sure, they would all be killed for what they'd discovered.

Andrew moved to the living room window, where he'd drawn the curtains.

He pulled them back just a sliver, so he could peer outside. The police car was still parked across the street. He looked again, closer this time.

The officer had parked in a place where the light didn't shine into the cab of the car, but it looked as though he was slumped over the steering wheel. He might be sleeping, but Andrew knew he couldn't assume that.

He hurried to Dean's room and spoke in a commanding voice. "Wake up, I think we got trouble."

His friend sat up with a start. "What's going on?"

"Watch Hope. I need to check on the patrol officer. I think he might have been knocked out."

Dean got out of bed and hurried to the living room. "Be careful. He may be trying to lure you out there."

"I am well aware of that. Please watch from the window in case I need backup." Andrew rushed toward the front door and stepped out into the darkness.

"Hope, wake up." Dean shook her shoulder.

Her eyes fluttered open. "What?" Fear sliced through her. "Where's Andrew?"

"He's outside. Something might be up with our protection," Dean told her. "Come on, I need to keep an eye you."

All the lights but one in the kitchen had been turned off. They hurried across the dark room and crouched at the front window. At first, when Hope lifted the bottom of the curtain and peered out, she couldn't see anything. The patrol car was shrouded in darkness.

Then Andrew emerged from the shadows and headed toward the car, looking side to side as he pulled his gun.

Jasper barked from the other side of the living room and padded toward the kitchen.

"Enough with the delay. I think we need to call this in. Get the police here." Dean stalked back toward his bedroom, probably to get his phone.

Her chest tightened as she watched Andrew

lean down to peer into the window and then open the car door.

When she looked out the window again, he was headed back toward the house. Though she could not see his face clearly, his body language communicated a sense of urgency. He stepped deliberately toward the house.

Dean was in the bedroom talking to the police.

A sort of thudding noise came from the kitchen. Her heart beat faster.

Jasper emerged from the kitchen, pacing and agitated. She reached out for the dog. "Was that you?"

The noise from the kitchen amplified. Some-one was in there throwing things around. Was it the assassin?

She reached for the door to get to Andrew just as Jason Zimmerman stepped into the living room.

"I see you've been busy." Jason raised his gun.

Dean stepped out of the bedroom just as the shot was fired. Hope dived for the floor and scrambled for the small amount of cover that the overstuffed chair provided.

Had Dean slipped back into the bedroom?

Andrew must have heard the gun fired from outside. She was feet away from the front door and the room was still dark.

She heard Jason's uneven footsteps. A light

came on in the living room. It was just a matter of time before she was found.

Andrew should have been at the door by now.

Another light went out.

A shot was fired in the direction of Dean's bedroom. He must have tried to sneak out to get to her.

Jasper barked.

Then she heard the sound of two men scuffling. She lifted her head above the arm of the chair. Andrew had come in through the back door and tackled Jason.

"Come one step closer and your friend gets it," Jason snarled.

When she peered above the arm of the chair, Dean stood with his hands in the air while the assassin held a gun to Andrew's head.

All the breath left her lungs.

"The police are on their way," Dean warned him.

"I'm sure I'll be okay." He poked Andrew with the gun. "Since I got collateral." He spoke to Andrew. "Back up nice and slow."

Jason led Andrew through the kitchen. The back door slammed against its frame.

Hope heard sirens in the distance as she rose to her feet and ran to the kitchen, where Jason had swept the table nearly bare of all the information they'd put together.

She moved to run after Jason and help Andrew, but Dean caught her. "He's armed, Hope. You are no match for him."

"I have to try after all Andrew has done for me!"

Dean wrapped an arm around her waist as she reached for the doorknob. "You'll only end up dead."

She struggled against his hold only for a moment. Dean was right, but the longing to run to Andrew, to try to help him, was overwhelming.

She stared at the blackness out the window.

Would the police get here in time to save Andrew?

TWENTY-ONE

Jason Zimmerman moved the gun from Andrew's head to his back as he swung him around and pushed him into the darkness. Andrew had dropped his gun in the scuffle.

Andrew knew two things. He needed to get the gun away from Zimmerman, and he needed to do it within seconds if he wanted to live.

Andrew planted his feet, pivoted and drove his knee into the hit man's stomach and then rammed a fist into his throat.

The move disoriented Zimmerman and left him choking for air but he held on to the gun.

Andrew dived for it. The gun went off in the air as the two men wrestled to the ground.

The police sirens seemed very far away.

Zimmerman was on top of him, pummeling his face. The gun must have fallen into the brush by the street.

The blows were disorienting as he fought off

unconsciousness. He grabbed the man's collar, pulled him closer and socked him in the jaw.

The sirens grew louder. Zimmerman stood up and ran toward a cluster of trees. Andrew pushed himself to his feet, swaying. He ran after him, leaping through the air and landing on the other man's back.

"You're not getting away." Even as he spoke, Andrew feared he would pass out from the blows to the head he'd received.

"Watch me."

His opponent was strong and agile. Undeterred, Andrew put all his weight on the other man's back, trying to hold him in place.

They were hidden by the trees. It might take the police a few minutes of searching before they were found. It was up to him to subdue Zimmerman and take him into custody.

The man angled his body. Andrew sought to keep him on his stomach with a neck hold, but Zimmerman managed to turn on his side and hit Andrew in the stomach. The assassin crawled out from under Andrew and stood up. Before Andrew could get to his feet, Jason's boot made contact with his jaw. The blow caused a vibration of pain through his head as his eyes watered.

By the time Andrew stood up, the perp had reached the white truck parked on the street. Andrew sprinted toward the truck just as Zimmerman swung the door open.

Andrew clamped his hands on the man's shoulders and yanked him away from the open truck door. Zimmerman turned and lunged at him, but Andrew was ready, striking the nerve in the larger man's neck.

Lights shone through the trees and two police officers appeared. Both with their weapons aimed.

Andrew held up his hands in surrender and stepped back. "This is the man you want."

The older officer stepped forward and cuffed Zimmerman.

"I'm sure you will be wanting my statement," Andrew said to the younger officer whom he recognized from earlier in the evening. "But I need to get back to the house."

The younger officer, who kept his gun on Zimmerman, nodded. The assassin shook his body like a dog holding a dead rabbit at being handcuffed but otherwise did not resist. He grinned at Andrew, showing his metal teeth. "This isn't over. Not by a long shot."

The threat sent a chill down Andrew's spine as he turned to go. The motorcycle assassin was still out there. He might even be watching. No doubt, the Queen Bee would be informed of Jason Zimmerman's arrest.

When he arrived back at the house, Hope burst out the front door to meet him. She fell into his arms. There were three police cars on the street in addition to the officer who had been assigned guard duty and had been knocked unconscious.

He took her into an embrace.

"I was so afraid something bad had happened to you." Deep affection permeated her words.

He relished how good it felt to hold her. "I'm okay, and Zimmerman is in custody."

She pulled away to look him in the eye. "That's wonderful. But he knows what we found out. He saw what we had spread out on that table."

Andrew nodded as his arms fell to his side. "Even though we haven't put together the whole picture, I've got to get in touch with the DEA, maybe through Julie or Agent Valdez, tell them what we figured out and turn the thumb drives and other things over."

"She'll find out, won't she, the Queen Bee, about Jason being caught and my brother's things?"

Andrew nodded. For vengeance alone, the Queen Bee would probably come down even harder on them. It might be that she would know that she was about to be exposed, and she would flee the country. No matter what, she was going to send people after Hope.

Andrew reached up and brushed his knuckles against Hope's cheek. He could not deny the intense feelings he had for her. "Who would have thought the head of the biggest drug syndicate in the western US could be taken down by a second-grade teacher?"

"It's not over yet," she cautioned.

"Agreed. But we are so much closer. We need to get more protection for you in a way that WITSEC can't find out. I'll see if my FBI friends can help me out."

While Jason was put in a police car, Andrew addressed one of the other officers who were standing around. "I think that our lives might still be in danger. Is there any way you could place someone outside for a while longer?"

"We'll see what we can do," said the officer. "You were in a bit of a fight. Don't you think you should be checked out medically?"

Andrew shook his head. "I'll be all right. I need to stay close to her."

Hope stood off to one side, waiting for him. They walked back to the house together. In the living room, Andrew picked up his gun where he'd dropped it.

They found Dean in the kitchen picking up the evidence Jason had swept to the floor. Jasper sat at his feet. Dean put a stack of papers that must have fallen out of a binder on the table. "That was wild. Like I said before, Andrew, never a dull moment when I'm around you."

Hope picked a thumb drive off the floor. "How much damage was done here?"

"Your brother's laptop doesn't work anymore," Dean answered.

"We still need to turn it over. Tech guys might still be able to salvage it." Andrew patted his friend's back. "Listen, Dean, that guy being taken into custody doesn't mean it's the end of the trouble for us. You've already done so much already."

"Are you kidding me? Feels like I'm back with the marshals again," said Dean. "I'm glad to help you out anyway I can."

"Sure am glad to have a friend like you." Andrew bear-hugged Dean.

They continued to try to sort the evidence they had gone through. Andrew stared at a headband that had the logo for the sports drink on it. It must have gotten tossed in one of the boxes they'd taken from the cabin by accident.

Still holding the headband, he sat down. "I think I saw things with this logo on it in one of the WITSEC administrative offices."

Hope took a chair as well. "But you don't remember who?"

He shook his head. "Some momentary interaction. That's why it's not solid in my memory. Maybe I poked my head into an office to ask a question. Or maybe the person was drinking from a cup with the logo on it. All I know is that when I saw this logo in your brother's things, I felt like I had seen it before."

"It must be one of those four names that Bryson had narrowed it down to," Hope mused.

"One of the people on there is a marshal who recently transferred to the New Mexico office and one is the case manager who handled your case. I think I would have remembered if I'd seen something like that in one of their offices."

"So that narrows it down to the two names you don't recognize." Hope stood up and studied the haphazard piles on the table. "Where is that piece of paper?"

"I kept it in my pocket." He pulled it out and read. "Loretta Eastman and James Marcus. Not ringing any bells for me...."

Hope shifted in her chair and ran her fingers through her hair in frustration. "What do we do now?"

"My number one priority is getting you to a safe place and quickly. As much as I appreciate his attitude, Dean does not need to live through another assault. And trust me, it will happen." He pulled his phone out. "I'm going to call Julie and Valdez and see if they know any agents in Wyoming who could help us with a secure location for you."

"And then what happens?"

"Once I know for sure that you're in a safe

place, I think I need to go back to the New Mexico offices and poke around. Try to see if I can jar my memory about where I saw that logo."

"But that will put you in danger and we'll be apart," she choked out.

"That's part of my job." He didn't want to be separated from her, either, but her going anywhere the leak would be walking into the lion's den. He wanted to make sure the Queen Bee's henchmen would not have access to this woman he cared about so deeply.

She covered his hand with her own. "Andrew, I'm so very afraid. I don't know what I would do if something bad happened to you."

He leaned in and kissed her, knowing that the fear was not unfounded and wanting more than anything to reassure her. But even he knew that his life was at risk.

Andrew's kiss warmed Hope down to her toes, and she longed to remain in his arms. As she pulled away and gazed deep into his eyes, it was clear how much they cared for each other. She saw, though, how impossible the situation was. He must see it, too. "We should stop kissing like that."

He pressed his hand on her cheek. "I know. Once you have your new placement, I won't be in your life. For me to even be your contact puts you at risk."

She closed her eyes. Relishing the tenderness of his touch, she covered his hand with hers. "It's a truth I am having a hard time with. Andrew... You mean so much to me."

He lifted his hand from her face and pushed his chair back, breaking the moment of connection between them, probably on purpose. Any fantasy of them being together even though both could admit their feelings was just that, a fantasy. After grabbing his phone, he stood up. "I'll make those calls." He retreated to the living room.

As she listened to the muffled conversation, Hope slumped in her chair. Tears pricked her eyes.

A whimper caused her to look down. Jasper was at her feet. He nudged her hand with his nose. She petted his soft head.

Dean stepped into the kitchen. "Why don't I fix you and Andrew something to eat before you take off."

"That would be nice." Hope rubbed Jasper's ear. "Your dog seems to know when I'm distressed."

Dean opened the refrigerator and pulled out several things. "Yeah, Jasper is pretty sensitive to the mood in the room. He'd do well as an emotional support animal. What is bothering you, beyond the obvious?"

She could still hear Andrew's voice in the next room as he made more calls. "Against our better judgment, Andrew and I have developed feelings for each other."

"Yeah, I kind of picked up on that." Dean threw something in the frying pan that made a sizzling sound. "First time since his wife died that I've seen him connect with a woman."

The aroma of hamburger cooking filled the air.

"Such a profound loss. I'm sure it gutted him." Perhaps what had drawn them together was the fact that they both had been ripped from safe worlds. They both had lost someone they loved. Probably not the best basis for a relationship.

Dean stepped away from the stove and opened the refrigerator to pull more items out. "All I know is that Andrew loves being a marshal. He'd never give it up."

The man's words seemed to echo in her mind. She resolved to appreciate the time she'd had with Andrew. The kisses and the hugs they'd shared had been unforgettable, but it couldn't happen again. She needed to let go of the idea that there could be anything more between them. Swallowing a lump in her throat, she pushed the notebooks and thumb drives to one side of the table so there would be room for them to eat.

Andrew stuck his head into the kitchen. "Smells nice in here."

"Thought you two might want to be functioning on a full stomach," Dean said.

Andrew sat down beside Hope. "It's all set up. Julia knew an agent who operates out of Cheyenne. He'll pick us up within an hour. The two of us will escort you to the safe house."

"What about all this evidence?" She pointed to the piles of notebooks and other items.

"That's the purview of the DEA." Andrew looked at Dean. "If you don't mind. They can't get someone here until tomorrow."

"I don't need the table." His friend shrugged. "I usually eat in the living room anyway."

"The guy from DEA is Mark Haloburg," Andrew added. "The DEA will be able to make more sense of it than we could and connect it with whatever other intel they've been able to gather on the Queen Bee."

"You'll be going with me to the safe house, then?" Her voice lilted up half an octave.

"Yes, we need all the manpower we can get to ensure a safe journey for you. I want to make sure the location we're taking you to is highly secure before I leave." He rested his hand on hers. "I'm not taking any chances."

The warmth of his touch soaked through her skin. "I appreciate all that you have done for me, Andrew." Making her voice sound as neutral as possible, she pulled her hand away.

She saw a flash of affection in Andrew's eyes before a curtain seemed to fall over his features.

They both knew they needed to sever the bond that had grown between them.

Dean pulled some buns out of a cupboard. "Okay, so tell me how you like your burgers. Cheese or no cheese, pickle, lettuce, tomato…" He turned and placed the ketchup and mustard on the table.

"All of that sounds good," Andrew told him.

"Same for me except no tomato," she said.

Dean laid out three plates, each with a bun and burger with melted cheese on it. He sliced the tomato and tore the lettuce, then placed them on the table. "Give me just a second to find the pickles, and we'll be ready to chow down."

After she put her toppings on, she took a bite of the juicy burger. They ate and gathered their few belongings together. Within the hour, a dark blue sedan pulled up to the street.

Andrew peered out the window. "I think that's our guy."

Hope stood beside him at the window. The police car with the officer was still parked outside. Andrew stepped outside to greet the man who had just gotten out of the car.

Dean stepped into the living room. Jasper was right behind him. "He's here, huh?"

"Yes, thank you for the good meals and hospitality. And most of all, the help in so many ways."

"No problem. Like I said before, life had been a little bit dull since I had to leave my job."

Andrew returned. "You ready to go?"

She nodded. Kneeling, she said goodbye to Jasper and gave Dean a hug. Andrew hugged his pal as well.

"When all this calms down, you and I have to put together a fishing trip."

"You got it, my friend," Dean said with a grin.

They headed outside to the car. Andrew sat in the back seat of the sedan with Hope. The FBI agent responded to the small talk Andrew attempted with one-word answers.

"Where are we going anyway?"

"Safe house is about twenty miles from here," the driver said. He pulled out onto the street and drove through the residential area toward the highway.

They had been on the highway for about ten minutes when Andrew's phone dinged. He pulled it out and read the text. Hope leaned toward him to see that the text was from Dean. Andrew's face blanched. His pulse throbbed on the side of his neck as his jaw tightened. He angled the phone so Hope could read the text.

Don't know who you are in the car with, but the FBI agent just showed up here. Also, I found a bugging device in the living room. Must have been placed there while I was tied up and Jason waited for you to show up.

Hope felt like she couldn't get a breath.

Andrew went to the notes part of his phone and typed in a two-word message.

Play along.

They were in a car with a man whose intent was to kill them.

TWENTY-TWO

Andrew steeled himself against the rising fear and willed his mind to focus on solutions. They needed to get out of this car and away from this man.

The sign on the side of the road said they were about to come to a town named Trout. "Can we stop at the next convenience store or rest stop? I forgot to go to the bathroom before we left. Too much coffee I guess."

"Sure," said the man behind the steering wheel.

Andrew's phone dinged. Dean again.

Where are you headed? We'll come for you.

Andrew's finger shook as he texted back.

Highway 25 just outside of Trout.

"You sure are getting a lot of texts," the driver remarked.

"Just trying to make some arrangements," Andrew said.

"What kind of arrangements?"

"Kind of an involved investigation I'm dealing with."

The driver slowed and then turned off the highway and headed up a forest service road.

Hope's voice faltered. "Where are we going?"

"A shortcut." The low-clearance sedan slowed over the rough road. They were going less than five miles an hour as the man tried to shift down. The sedan was not suited for such a rough road.

Andrew pulled Hope close and whispered in her ear, "Jump."

It took only seconds to scoot to the door and push it open. Andrew jumped and rolled.

The car stopped.

He rose to his feet and scanned the area for Hope. She came around the side of the car just as the driver leaped out.

The man had pulled his gun.

Andrew grabbed Hope's hand. Shots were fired as they ran into the trees. They weren't that far from the highway. Once they were hidden by the forest, Andrew turned to head down the mountain.

While he pulled his own gun and braced for more gunfire, none came. The driver had not followed them into the trees. "He must be going to meet us at the bottom of the road." The guy could get there faster in the car than they could on foot, assuming he could get turned around and not get stuck. "Let's go this way."

"But he might be waiting for us down there," she said.

"Let's try and prevent another encounter."

Andrew led them sideways to try to come out on the highway as far away from the forest service access as possible. After they'd run to the point of being winded, he stopped and pulled his phone out. He phoned Dean.

He didn't wait for his friend to say anything. "We took a detour on a forest service access road right before we reached Trout. Killer is most likely searching for us in his car."

Dean responded, "Getting there as fast as we can."

As they worked their way down the mountain, Andrew heard the occasional rush of a car going by on the road. After walking for a few minutes more, he could see the highway through the thinning trees.

There was no way to calibrate exactly where they were on the road.

"You stay back," he said to Hope. "I'm going to poke my head out and see if I can spot a mile marker or some kind of landmark to give Dean a better idea of where to find us."

Nodding, Hope stepped toward a tree.

Andrew eased down the hill until he could see the road. He saw nothing but trees and forest. The best location he could give Dean was how close they'd been to Trout. Just before he stepped back into the trees, he saw the sedan go by on the highway. The guy had made it back down and was looking for them.

He hurried back to where Hope waited. "Let's just keep moving and stay in touch with Dean."

Fifteen minutes went by as they hiked deeper into the forest but always with an idea of where the forest service turnoff was. Dean called to say he and the agent had just passed the sign indicating how close Trout and the other towns were. "We're looking for the forest service turnoff road now."

"We're not too far from there," Andrew told him. They made their way back to the road. While they hid in the trees, he listened for the sound of a car headed up the road.

The man in the sedan must be close by watching and waiting as well.

A car Andrew didn't recognize but one that was built for off-road travel eased by. Both he and Hope remained hidden and watched until the car stopped.

A text came in from Dean.

We're here.

They ran to the car. Dean got out and greeted them. Once they were secure in the back seat, his friend introduced the man with the buzz cut behind the wheel.

"This is the real Agent Phillips."

The man nodded. He rolled up the forest service road until he found a place to turn around. "My guess is we're going to be followed once we're back out on the road."

"Yes," Andrew confirmed. "The guy is driving a car not suited for a rough road like this. But I suspect he's watching, waiting for us to come out on the highway."

"He's not going to give up." Hope's voice faltered as she pressed her hand over her heart and closed her eyes.

Andrew patted her other hand hoping to offer support.

"Well, we're not going directly to the safe house, then." Agent Phillips pulled back out onto the highway. "And we'll get in touch with highway patrol, see if they can take him in."

"Let's hope they catch him," Hope whispered.

As they rolled down the road, Andrew gave Agent Phillips a description of the sedan so he could phone it in to highway patrol.

They were within a mile of Trout when a motorcycle came up behind them.

"This might be trouble," Andrew cautioned. "Prepare to be fired at."

The motorcycle had already slipped into the turning lane when the sedan appeared as well, easing toward them from behind.

"Duly noted." Agent Phillips increased his speed, trying to outrun the motorcycle. Andrew could see the city limits up ahead.

The motorcycle assassin raised his gun, fired and sped away. The shot went through the driver's side window.

Dean clutched his shoulder as his voice filled with anguish. "I'm hit."

Hope let out a gasp and lurched in her seat.

Andrew felt like he'd been punched in the gut. He leaned forward to offer his friend comfort. "Hang in there."

They had entered the city of Trout.

"They have a hospital here," Agent Phillips assured them. He zoomed through the city streets.

Dean's hand was bloody and shaking.

"Let me put pressure on the wound," Andrew said.

They arrived at the hospital and hurried through the ER. When Andrew glanced back at the hospital parking lot, he saw the sedan pull into place with a highway patrol car arriving seconds later to take the driver into custody. But the danger was far from over.

The motorcycle assassin was still out there.

Hope's heart squeezed tight as the ER crew put Dean on a stretcher and rushed him out of view down a hallway.

All the color had drained from Andrew's face. She reached for his hand and squeezed.

"This wasn't his fight." He stared at the blood on his own hands. "And yet he was willing to help because he's my friend. I don't know what I would do if he doesn't make it."

There was nothing she could say to ease Andrew's anguish. Instead, she guided him toward a chair and invited him to sit. Agent Phillips paced in front of the glass ER doors before coming to sit down beside them.

At least the driver of the sedan would not come after them.

Hope noticed a security guard walk through the waiting room.

The three of them waited for hours for news of Dean. Andrew rose from his chair and paced, then sat back down. After losing Bryson, he was probably undone by what had happened to Dean.

Hope sat beside Andrew wishing there was something she could say. Agent Phillips still watched the parking lot outside.

A nurse emerged from the long hallway to tell them that Dean was out of surgery but not yet awake.

Andrew rose to his feet. "Could I—would it be all right if I stayed with him in his room?"

"Sure," said the nurse.

"I'll go with you," Hope offered.

Andrew had clearly been wrecked by Dean being shot. She knew no way to ease his pain but to be with him.

After they filled in Phillips on what was going on, the agent promised to keep watch in the waiting area. Then they followed the nurse down a hallway. "He's in room four."

They entered the dim room where Dean remained unconscious. Both of them scooted the chairs closer to the hospital bed.

"We need to pray for your friend," Hope whispered.

Andrew nodded.

She held his hands and closed her eyes. "Lord Jesus, we pray that Dean would recover from this wound." She squeezed his hands before letting go.

She didn't know what else to do. The hours ticked by and day turned to night. They took turns staying awake.

Hope rose to her feet to stretch. "Are you hungry? I can go to the cafeteria to get us something to eat if they're open. Otherwise there might be a vending machine."

Still half-asleep, Andrew rubbed his eyes. "Yes, I could use some food." He glanced at Dean, who remained unresponsive, then he stood up and walked toward her. "Thanks for staying with me. It means a lot."

"No problem." She fell into his arms, hoping to comfort him. "I know what a good friend he is." She pulled away, wishing the hug could last longer.

She stepped out into the hallway, trying to remember if she'd seen a sign for a cafeteria.

A woman in a nurse's smock who had been standing in the hallway came toward her. "You look lost. Can I help you?"

"I thought I remembered seeing a sign for the cafeteria."

"This place is a bit of a labyrinth. Follow me," said the nurse.

Hope followed the woman down a hallway. The signs indicated that these were the offices for maintenance and engineering.

"Are you sure we're going the right way?" Hope slowed down, staring at the back of the woman's head.

"You work here long enough, you learn all the shortcuts," the nurse told her.

Though she couldn't pinpoint the reason for her unease, she turned to get away.

The other woman grabbed her. "Where do you think you're going?" She pulled a needle from her pocket and jabbed it into Hope's shoulder.

A man, the motorcycle assassin, appeared out of nowhere. He wore the uniform of an EMT. Hope was fully aware of what was happening, though her body was paralyzed and she was powerless to fight back. She was loaded onto a stretcher and pushed down the hallway.

The woman leaned over Hope. "We can't kill you here. There are too many people around. We need to take you somewhere more secluded."

The dead eyes and nondescript features of the Queen Bee stared down at Hope.

She tried to respond but the muscles in her throat did not work.

"You've caused quite a bit of trouble for me," the Queen Bee said.

The ringleader had had plenty of time to get here while she and Andrew watched over Dean. She may have only been hours away since her operation was all over the western US. Hope was wheeled down a different hallway. Lights and ceiling tiles clicked by above her.

The Queen Bee leaned over her and smiled. "It will be my pleasure to personally finish this job myself."

TWENTY-THREE

Seconds after Hope left the room, Andrew had a sinking feeling in his gut. She shouldn't be wandering the hospital alone. He hurried out into the empty hallway. His chest squeezed tight. Something was wrong.

He phoned Agent Phillips but got no answer. Andrew ran toward the ER entrance. The agent was nowhere in sight.

He addressed the woman behind the counter. "The man with the buzz cut. Where did he go?"

The woman shook her head. "Not sure."

Andrew noticed a small waiting room off to the side. When he stepped inside, he found Agent Phillips unconscious but alive. Andrew ran out to the main reception area. "There's a man in there who needs medical attention."

He stared out the glass doors where a familiar-looking blond man in an EMT uniform loaded a patient into an ambulance. The doors closed.

"Call the police. I think one of your ambulances was just stolen."

Andrew burst outside just as the ambulance pulled away. Since when does an ambulance take a patient away from a hospital? Hope must be in there.

He found a man who had just pressed the key to lock his truck. Andrew showed his marshal ID. "I need your vehicle."

The ambulance was at the edge of the hospital parking lot.

The man handed Andrew his key. He jumped in the truck and drove toward where the ambulance had just turned down a street.

He pressed the gas as the ambulance accelerated toward the edge of town and headed up a dark, unlit road. He had to stop them to save Hope. The truck had some horsepower, so he pressed the gas pedal to the floor and rammed into the back bumper of the ambulance.

The collision only made the ambulance go faster, then swing sideways and stop in the road. He could see now that the driver was the motorcycle assassin. The assassin rolled down the window and raised a gun in the direction of Andrew's windshield.

Andrew shifted to Reverse. Several shots were fired in his direction.

Using the door as a shield, he jumped out of

the truck, pulled his gun and aimed toward the motorcycle assassin. The man ducked down in the cab of the ambulance.

Andrew took cover behind a bush that was alongside the road.

The back of the ambulance doors burst open and the assailant jumped out, advancing toward the truck. The guy thought Andrew was still in there.

The open doors of the ambulance revealed a woman bent over the person on the stretcher with a knife in her hand.

No. He had to get to her in time.

Andrew scanned the darkness. When he spotted what he thought was movement coming toward him, he took his shot, praying he'd hit his target.

Knowing he risked being shot himself if the assassin was still out there. He didn't care. All that mattered was saving Hope. he rushed to the front bumper of the ambulance and circled around to the open doors.

He raised his gun when he saw the woman about to plunge a knife into Hope. "Put it down."

The woman whirled around, eyes ablaze with rage. Andrew fired a shot just as the woman got behind the wheel of the ambulance and drove away with the back doors wide open.

The ambulance rumbled away with the

stretcher bouncing on the bumpy road. Andrew got into his borrowed truck and followed it. The road wound down toward a river.

The ambulance stopped and the woman got out, running alongside the river. Andrew could hear sirens in the distance as he jumped out and pursued the fleeing woman. He caught up with her and tackled her.

She drew a knife on him before he could reach his gun. This had to be the Queen Bee. She slashed the knife in the air. He stepped back to avoid being cut, but dived in right after, grabbing the hand that didn't hold a weapon.

She sliced the knife across his shoulder. Pain coursed through his body as he reached to get her other wrist, applying pressure on the nerves in her wrist.

They were face-to-face. "Drop the weapon," he commanded.

She angled from side to side and tried to kick him before the knife fell to the ground and he was able to twist her hands behind her.

Now that he saw the Queen Bee close up, he knew now who the leak was in the WITSEC office. The two women resembled each other. They must be cousins or even sisters. Queen Bee might even have planted her there on purpose to get at other people who betrayed the cartel.

The police car had arrived at the ambulance.

He led the woman who had caused so much heartache for Hope to the police so they could cuff her. The motorcycle assassin, who appeared to have been shot in the arm, was taken away in an ambulance that was called.

Andrew jumped into the ambulance where Hope was strapped to the stretcher. She looked at him with recognition in her eyes but did not move.

He brushed his fingers over her forehead. "They drugged you with a paralytic."

Something in her eyes communicated yes.

"It's over, she's in custody and I know who the leak is." He gently cradled her face in his hand. "You did it. You took down the Queen Bee. The leak will be picked up soon enough and you get your life back."

Her eyes glistened with tears.

Arrangements were made for Hope to be transported back to the hospital to be made comfortable until the drug wore off. Andrew spent the rest of the night moving from Hope's room to Dean's.

In the early morning hours, Dean opened his eyes.

"Hey." Dean's weak voice floated across the room to Andrew, who was half-asleep. He sat up straighter and leaned so he could touch his friend's shoulder.

"Welcome back," he said. "You missed all the excitement."

"Oh, I'd say I had plenty." Dean tried to laugh but it was clear that caused pain.

"She's in custody. The Queen Bee," Andrew assured him. "And I know who the leak is."

"So it's all over? Hope will be set up somewhere with a new identity?"

Andrew nodded. "A new life and identity. We can't take any chances. The cartel is substantially less powerful with the Queen Bee in custody, but that doesn't mean they won't still come after Hope for revenge."

"That probably means you don't get to see her again."

The sadness of that statement sank into Andrew's bones. "True. It puts her at risk for me to be her contact even as a marshal."

The only way to keep her safe was for him not to be in her life. Though the idea ripped him in two, he knew that was how it had to be.

Hope had not expected the airplane that would take her to her new life to be so small. It looked like maybe it could hold ten people. How would it take her all the way from Wyoming to Seattle and then Alaska, where her new identity had been set up?

The marshal who would escort her was a lean

older man with white-and-silver hair who reminded her of the actor Sam Elliott. Though he said his name was Thomas.

Once the paralytic had worn off in the hospital, she'd only been given a brief chance to say goodbye to Andrew before being taken to a safe house. Even as he kissed her and wished her the best life ever, she knew that she loved him. She'd fallen hard for the quiet man who was reluctant to reveal his heart or the pain of past loss. But he'd opened up to her and she'd found him to be caring and protective.

Knowing she wouldn't see Andrew again was the hardest part about the new placement.

Weeks passed while the leak in WITSEC was arrested, and a new identity was put together for her.

The other passengers began to board. Thomas ushered her toward the exterior stairs that led into the small airplane.

A man emerged from behind the parked airplanes holding an envelope.

"Looks like we got one more passenger," Thomas said.

She glanced around. "What do you mean one more passenger?"

As the man came out of the shadows, she saw that it was Andrew and he was holding an envelope.

Her heart leaped with joy just to see him one more time. Had he come to say goodbye?

She rushed toward him, feeling her spirit soar. "Andrew. I'm glad you came."

Thomas moved away so they could have a private moment.

"It's good to see you smile, Hope." Andrew reached a hand out to touch her arm as his voice tinged with affection.

"I'm just glad you came to see me off." She wanted to fall into his arms. But breaking free of his embrace would be too much for her to endure. Seeing him was bittersweet, knowing that he would not stay.

He shook his head. "It's more than that. I'm hoping this isn't goodbye."

She shook her head, not understanding.

Andrew held up the envelope. "This is me. The *new* me in here. It took some doing and coordination between the marshal districts. I wasn't sure if we were going to make it on time."

Hope glanced over at the plane, where the last passenger had boarded. "What are you talking about?"

"We put together a new identity for me so that I can enter the program with you. I would be going with you to Alaska as your husband, if you are open to that."

Hope's mind reeled as confusion battled with

a blossoming hope. "You mean for extra protection?"

"Of course I would protect you but that is not what I'm saying. I want to be with you for real and forever. We can disappear together." He stepped closer, locking his gaze on her.

When he looked at her that way, warmth sank into her skin despite the chill wind. Andrew wanted to be with her! The notion elated her, but it would be such a sacrifice. "Oh, Andrew. You'd be giving up your job."

He pressed his hand against her cheek. "The problem is in the weeks that have gone by, I can't picture a life without you. You matter more to me than any job. Will you marry me?"

She looked up at him, seeing the devotion shining in his eyes. They could have a life together. "Yes, Andrew. I will marry you."

He gathered her into his arms, swung her around, then set her on the ground and kissed her.

Hope pulled back from the kiss to look at this man who had given up so much to be with her. She could picture a life of adventure and growing old with him.

"I love you so much, Hope." A smile graced his face and he leaned in and kissed her again, then whispered in her ear. "You have made me the happiest man in the whole world."

And she was the happiest woman in the whole world. "I love you, too," she whispered back.

Thomas stepped forward. "I hate to break this up. But the plane is waiting."

Andrew held Hope in a sideways hug. "Here's to our new life together."

As they stepped toward the plane and headed up the stairs, Hope realized she could not imagine any greater joy than to spend her life with Andrew as his wife.

* * * * *

Dear Reader,

I hope you enjoyed the exciting and dangerous adventure that Hope and Andrew embarked on in order to find a place of safety and love. As I wrote this book, I thought a great deal about God's protection and presence. Most of us will not go through the harrowing dangers that Hope and Andrew faced, but all of us will have suffering in our lives. I know for me when trials happen, it's easy to think that God has lost my phone number. God's protection does not mean that bad things won't happen to us. It does mean that He is with us even if we don't think so. The Bible verse I picked at the beginning of this book was from an abundance of verses that remind us that God will not abandon us. Romans 8: 38 39 tells us that nothing can separate us from the love of God. In many ways, I think God's protection is His presence. He never leaves us or forsakes us. And like the verse in Joshua says, "For the Lord God is with thee withersoever thou goest."

Blessings
Sharon Dunn